Charmzy
A Leprechaun's Tale

MICHELLE L. LEBRON

Copyright © 2024 Michelle L. LeBron

No part of this book may be reproduced or transmitted in any form or by any means, electronic or mechanical, including photocopying, recording or by any information storage or retrieval system, without written permission from the author and the publisher, except for the inclusion of a brief quotation in a review.

Edited by Marie Barteld

"To my children, Ireland, Madison, and Tristan-
may your dreams soar as high as the boundless sky
and your imaginations light up the world with wonder.
May your journeys be filled with magic, hope,
and infinite possibilities. Always believe in yourselves a
nd the extraordinary within you."

Prologue
The Legacy of the Clovers

Long before the first whispers of the rainbow's gold and magic spread across the lands, the Cloverborn family was entrusted with a sacred duty. The mystical angel, Christel, and other ethereal beings from the celestial realm descended to earth to select a guardian who would protect the enchanted rainbows, the divine source of immense power. Each color of the rainbow represents nature, beauty, and the well-being of all living things on Earth.

In their divine wisdom, these ethereal beings chose the Cloverborn ancestors, a noble family known for their purity of heart and unwavering loyalty. As a covenant between Celestial Realms and Earth, the Cloverborns were gifted the rare and potent magic of the Clovers—a power unlike any other. This power was drawn from the legendary four-leaf clovers, which held the essence of the rainbow's magic, granting protection, healing, and foresight. These Clovers not only connected the Cloverborns to the Celestial Realm but made them the rightful guardians of the rainbow, ensuring that its powers would be used for good and shielding it from those who would misuse it.

For generations, the Cloverborns honored their agreement by safeguarding the magic and keeping the opening of the rainbow hidden from those driven by greed and corruption. Yet, with light comes darkness, and in this case, a rival family, the Malrends. Their name "mal" stems from the Latin word for bad and evil while the meaning of "rend" is to tear things apart. The Malrends, driven by jealousy and hunger for power, sought to steal the rainbow's magic and use it to control all realms. Their treachery and dark magic disrupted the balance, and a fierce conflict ensued between the two bloodlines.

In a climactic battle, Charmzy's grandfather, Ciaran Cloverborn, led the fight to stop the Malrend ancestors, Madison and Winfred's predecessors. The battle was fierce and filled with loss on both sides, but Ciaran managed to stop the Malrends before they could fully harness the power of the rainbow. However, the cost of that victory left scars on the Cloverborn family, and Ciaran mysteriously disappeared into the Hemlock Woods, never to return home again.

As generations passed, the Malrends' ambition never faded. And now, with Charmzy as the last of the Cloverborn bloodline, the legacy of the Clovers rests upon his shoulders as the battle between good and evil, light and shadow, begins anew.

Introduction

Along time ago, there lived a young and spirited leprechaun named Charmzy. Like any leprechaun in the village, he adorned himself in green knickers, buckled shoes, a white buttoned shirt, and a distinguished, black-buckled top hat. His slender frame boasted fair skin, blue eyes, and a radiant smile that revealed charming dimples.

Charmzy's youthful days were filled with tales, especially those that spoke of a mythical pot of gold awaiting discovery beyond the rainbow that arched over the Woods of Hemlock. Reminiscing about his childhood at the tender age of three, Charmzy often embarked on walks to Swan Pond with his grandmother, Lucy.

During these strolls, the pond would come alive with reflections of light, courtesy of a nearby candy store displaying vibrantly-colored lollipops tied up in iridescent cellophane wrap. These lollipops cast an array of rainbow colors onto the pond. Enchanted by the shimmering hues of the rainbow, young Charmzy would attempt to walk on the water's surface, dreaming of capturing the elusive pot of gold. But his endeavors ended with arms floundering in the air as he found himself submerged in the pond, crying out to his grandmother, "I did not get the gold!"

Amused by her grandson's antics, Grandmother Lucy would chuckle and dispel the fanciful notion.

"Charmzy, there is no gold over the rainbow. It is only a fairytale," she assured him.

Undeterred, Charmzy insisted, "No, Grandmother, they told me there is gold over the rainbow."

Grandmother Lucy inquired, "Who told you this, Charmzy?" to which he replied with youthful innocence, "The men in the tavern, Grandmother. I overheard their tales of gold in the Woods of Hemlock."

Letting out a deep belly laugh, Grandmother Lucy scolded him playfully, "Oh, Charmzy, do not listen to them. They are old drunken fools with dreams as wild as the stories they tell."

And so, the whimsical tales of a young leprechaun's quest for gold over the rainbow became woven into the fabric of Charmzy's enchanting childhood.

Chapter One
Tavern Whispers

Once upon a time, there was a curious and precocious young leprechaun named Charmzy. Slightly taller than the average leprechaun, he had fiery red hair that hung in loose waves below his ears and the bluest eyes anyone in his village had ever seen. Charmzy spent his days running through Dalkey Village, helping his elderly neighbors in hopes of receiving something sweet in return.

"Good afternoon, Mrs. Sullivan. Let me help you with your groceries," Charmzy said. He stretched out his long arms to reach the bags and lifted them up the entry stairs to Mrs. Sullivan's flat.

"Why, aren't you the most charming boy in this village!" Mrs. Sullivan exclaimed. Charmzy placed the grocery bags on the table and asked if she needed further assistance.

"No, Charmzy, I'm good. But wait a minute, I have something for you," Mrs. Sullivan said, reaching for her purse and pulling out a shiny coin. "This might be enough for you to buy something from the sweet shop."

"Thank you, Mrs. Sullivan," Charmzy said. He slowly closed the door behind him and then jumped down the stairs to the sidewalk, racing towards the sweet shop.

Charmzy, now ten years old, loved his favorite candy shop in the Village of Dalkey. As he ran, he heard laughter from a nearby tavern.

The sounds of amusement came from a group of people chanting, "Gold and rainbows! Gold! Rainbows!"

Charmzy came to a halt, peering inside the crack of the door. The cozy atmosphere of the village tavern, filled with laughter and the scent of ale, captivated him. He leaned closer in and cupped his left ear with his hand to catch every word of a captivating tale that promised to alter the course of his life forever.

Inside he saw an elderly gentleman dressed in a white shirt and faded brown overalls with frayed edges. His long, well-groomed white beard flowed down his chest, giving him a distinguished and wise appearance. Despite his age, his eyes were bright and alert, and his face was etched with deep wrinkles as he told stories of a life well-lived.

The elder continued, "Listen here. You must travel to the Woods of Hemlock and search for a vast, desolate space in the shape of a perfectly symmetrical circle. Amidst the barren landscape stands a singular tree trunk, long and slender, shaped like an angel. This angel will bestow the key to unlock the greatness of riches beyond your dreams." Then he exclaimed, "Over the rainbow to the gold!"

The men chanted again, "Rainbows! Gold! Rainbows and gold!"

Charmzy was intrigued and his eyes brightened at the possibility of gold. He thought to himself, "If I can get that gold, I can help my family and the people in my village."

The noisy chatter of men filled the dimly-lit tavern as they gulped down their ale and cider.

At the far end of the bar, one of the Irishmen shouted, "An angel! Tell us more! Will she use her angel wings to fly you over the rainbow to the gold?"

His words were met with uproarious laughter. Amidst the commotion, the elderly man spoke up, his voice firm and resolute. "Listen carefully, my friends. This is no joke! This beautiful angel holds the key to the Hemlock Rainbow which has within it mounds of glittering gold, enough to fill a king's castle from the ground to the top of the turret."

Charmzy crept inside the tavern and hid behind a bulky man seated on a chair. As he crouched behind the man, he listened intently to the story.

The men paused and began gathering around the elder. One man, with his belly protruding from the bottom of his red shirt, asked, "How do I get the key from the angel?"

Suddenly, a tiny old man hunched over with a walking stick appeared from behind a large table. The hump on his back was shaped like a camel's, not one hump but two.

His gray hair was scattered over the top of his head to camouflage his baldness and a rotten tooth hung off the side of his lip. The small man looked up at the elder and said, "Tell me more, old man."

The elder seemed to disagree with being called old. He looked down at the hunchbacked man and said, "Tell you what?"

"Tell me how to get the key to the gold," the hunchback asked.

"I can't say anymore," the elder replied.

The men began to yell in anger and pushed towards him. The hunchbacked man raised his walking stick and shouted, "Hold on there, young men!"

He turned his head upward, directly under the elder's chin, and said in a slow, soft tone, "What will it take for you to give us the keys to the gold?"

The elder tapped his fingers below his lip, and then, as though a light bulb had been lit in his mind, he stood up straight. "I'm happy to share the details, though I need something in return, as I'm not capable at my 'old age'"—looking sarcastically down at the hunchback—"to travel for the gold. Some gratuities for my knowledge would be greatly appreciated."

"Alright then," the hunchback shouted, "pay up, men!" The hunchback pulled out a shiny coin from his pocket and the other men followed suit, filling the elder's pouch until he was content.

"Alright, fellas, gather around and listen carefully." The men pulled into a tight circle around him.

"When you come across the Hemlock Circle, you will immediately know it's the correct spot. You will see a tall and majestic tree, its trunk twisted and gnarled like the outstretched fingers of an ancient giant. Intricate images are etched into its bark, each representing a unique story waiting to be told. The delicate folds of the angel's dress billow in the breeze. As the sun sets, the tree takes on an ethereal glow, as if it is alive with divine energy. It seems to guard the memories of what was once a beautiful forest, now reduced to torched trees and little life."

The man in the red shirt asked again, "How do I get the key from the angel if she is frozen inside the tree?"

The elder began to circle the men, his hand upon his chin, looking down at the tavern floor. "Well, it's not so simple—but you can start by standing atop the tree trunk and singing out loud for the angel to appear."

A man with crossed eyes and two missing front teeth caught everyone's attention. He stuttered, "Well, well . . . what's the song?" When the elder announced that he was a gifted singer, the cross-eyed man looked at him surprised. So, the elder then offered to sing the tune. The men gathered even closer around the long-bearded man who then stood up, cleared his throat, and began to sing:

> Christel, the angel, in the neon glow,
> Guide me to where dreams grow.
> Over the rainbow to the gold so bright
> On this starry night.

A short, chubby leprechaun with a bushy beard and eyes full of eagerness declared his determination to find the Hemlock Circle.

"Piece of cake! I can do this," he exclaimed. "I'll embark on this journey tomorrow and find this angel." As he pulled down his vest, his front pocket revealed a golden pocket watch. He checked the time and announced that he would set out just after dawn.

Sporting a wide grin, he called out, "Who will join me in the hunt for gold?"

The elder said he had heard of many adventurers who had attempted to reach Hemlock Circle but never returned. He said there were two significant challenges they had to face.

Standing tall in the center of the Irishmen, he told them, "First, an immense evil guards the rainbow and prevents anyone from getting close to it."

The elder did not know what form this evil took but had heard stories of brave souls who tried to fight it and failed. Some said it was a fierce dragon while others believed it was an evil spirit.

"Second," the elder continued, "the gold at Hemlock Circle is only for the chosen one."

Though the elder did not know all of the criteria used to choose the person, it was said that the chosen one was pure of heart and selfless. The stout, short-bearded leprechaun asked, "And how will we recognize the chosen one?" The men stood before the elder, eager to hear his words.

"If you are the chosen one," he began, his voice carrying the weight of years of experience, "Angel Christel will appear and lead you to the gold."

The men exchanged glances, unsure of what this meant or which one among them could be the chosen one. The elder's words caused the Irishmen to pause and ponder their next move.

The men individually questioned whether they truly embodied the qualities of the chosen one or if there was someone else better suited among them. They reflected on their past shortcomings in demonstrating kindness and purity. As for Angel Christel, they pondered whether she would even recognize kindness and purity if they were presented to her. They did, though, understand the importance of thoughtful consideration before proceeding further towards the Woods of Hemlock. That evening in the tavern, seven of the men engaged in meaningful discussions and began planning their expedition to the Woods of Hemlock.

The story set Charmzy's mind ablaze with visions of glistening treasures and the delectable treats he could buy as he inched out of the tavern. Charmzy then rushed into the candy shop just before closing. Mrs. O'Conner, the shop's owner, greeted him. "Why, hello, Charmzy! Lucky for you, I still have three minutes until I lock up, so have a quick look."

Mrs. O'Conner was counting out her cash register when Charmzy piped up, "I already know what I want." Mrs. O'Conner lifted her head away from the register and propped her elbow up on the counter. Her chin rested beneath her closed hand and she smiled widely, giving her full attention to her customer. "Well, what will you be having?" she asked.

"Those chocolate gold coins." Charmzy pointed to the high shelf behind the counter where they sat in a glass jar. She reached up and opened it, handing him some of the chocolate coins. Charmzy rushed out of the candy shop, gobbling them down along with big dreams of one day capturing Hemlock Rainbow's gold.

Meanwhile, back at the tavern, the bearded elder bid farewell to the tavern's patrons and departed, followed closely by a hunched figure. In the dimness of gray skies in a back alley, the hunchback shed his burdensome humps and straightened up.

"Those sandbags were a real burden," he muttered before asserting, "I'll take half the profits." Maintaining his composure, the elder handed over a share of the coins.

"And what of the tale of the rainbow and gold?" inquired the hunchback.

"Pure fantasy, my friend," the elder chuckled. "A whimsical dream from my youth while I lay asleep in the darkened Woods of Hemlock. I then spun my dream into a profitable yarn over the years."

"And what about the darkness you spoke of in the Woods of Hemlock?" the hunchback pressed for answers.

"Ah, there is some truth to that," the elder conceded. "I was young and scared when I sensed something ominous nearby in the darkness. At daylight, I woke up next to a tree that resembled an angel. That was all. Just a figment of my imagination. But I have no intention of going back to those woods. To put it bluntly, I was scared out of my boots!"

With that acknowledgment, the two men shook hands, and the partnership ended as they went their separate ways.

Chapter Two
The Seven Irishmen

Charmzy savored his breakfast the following day as he peered out the kitchen window. He watched with fascination as the men from the evening before at the tavern began to gather. They were preparing for their journey into the mysterious Woods of Hemlock, hoping to be the chosen one to find the legendary gold. With a deep sigh, Charmzy's grandmother placed her arm around his shoulder and together they peered out the window. The overcast sky and the silence in the air seemed to foreshadow that something was about to go wrong.

Grandma Lucy's eyes conveyed a sense of worry as she said, "This isn't going to go well."

"Why will it not go well, Grandmother?"

"Well, my little Charmzy, as I've said before, there is no such thing as gold over the rainbow. But there is evil and wickedness in those woods. So, it would be best if you always stayed clear of it, Charmzy. I don't believe those tales, you hear me?" she said.

"Grandmother, I hear you," Charmzy said. But his expression gave away his disappointment.

Lucy noticed the look on Charmzy's face and sat across the table from him, looking directly into his eyes.

She repeated her question, "Charmzy, can you promise me that you will always stay in Dalkey and never venture into those woods away from your mother?" Charmzy promised his grandmother he would do as his grandmother suggested.

Then Lucy stood up, walked around the table, and hugged Charmzy from behind as he ate breakfast.

As his grandmother walked out of the kitchen, his mother, Nadella, entered to grab a quick bite before heading out to work.

"Goodbye, my sweetness," she said to Charmzy, kissing his forehead before leaving.

Charmzy watched from the kitchen window as the seven Irishmen armed themselves with axes, bows, and arrows, prepared for any danger they might face in the dense woods. The village women had packed sacks of food for their husbands' long journey into the unknown.

The men then lined up and marched towards the woods, their voices ringing out in unison as they sang, "We are off to find the Angel, the beautiful, beautiful Angel, because of all the colorful, wonderful, glistening gold she will bestow on us."

They drifted into the woods, never to be seen again, apart from a leprechaun named Ivan who returned after two days in the woods.

Ivan was different from the other leprechauns in the village. He was taller with mighty strength in his arms and legs that ran at the speed of light. He would place bets to take down any man in an arm-wrestling match and was known to be the fastest runner in the village.

Ivan returned to the village in a terrified state, struggling to catch his breath, his lips blistered from the cold wind.

He rarely spoke about the horror he witnessed as he was there for only a moment before he bolted away, leaving his fellow leprechauns behind. He said he never found out what became of them. Ivan told the villagers what little he could remember. A bright, sunlit sky suddenly turned dark gray. A voice spoke gibberish that he assumed was a spell being cast. Then chaos erupted as several cyclones materialized out of nowhere and descended upon the group of men. In seconds the men were engulfed in a violent storm with heavy rain and winds spinning at high speeds.

Suddenly, one of the cyclones grabbed the group's leader with incredible force and lifted him off the ground towards the sky. At that point, Ivan darted back to Dalkey Village and didn't look back to see what happened to the rest of the group. The image of the cyclones falling from the sky and wreaking havoc on the men was forever etched in his mind.

Following the disappearance of the Irishmen in the woods, the leprechauns in the village decided against searching for them as they feared they might face the same fate.

The families of the missing men grieved their loss and the village was enveloped in a somber mood for quite some time. A few of the villagers continued to question Ivan, who was the last person to have seen the missing men, hoping to get clearer answers.

However, all they received was a shaky response from Ivan who kept repeating the same words over and over: "Cyclones, evil sky, gone." His response raised more questions than it answered, leaving the villagers to wonder what had happened to the missing men.

The curiosity Charmzy had about the mysterious Woods of Hemlock and its rainbow remained. However, he couldn't shake off his grandmother's warning about the dangers lurking there and Ivan's face which was full of fear.

After the Irishmen were lost, Lucy continued to paint a vivid picture of the woods, describing it as a dark and treacherous place full of thieves, witches, warlocks, and impurity. She even went as far as to say that the woods were cursed and that the darkness would consume anyone who dared to enter.

Despite his desire to explore the woods and discover if there was any truth to the tales of gold, Charmzy knew better than to defy his grandmother. With a heavy heart, he promised her time and time again that he would never venture into the woods.

As Charmzy grew older, time seemed to fly by. The days turned to weeks, and the weeks turned to months, until finally, he was fifteen years old. He would lay in his bed with flashes of his father showing him something, though he could never see it clearly. In these glimpses of his toddler years, he saw his grandmother standing beside the door, watching as his father whispered into his ear. However, Charmzy was not sure what was in those whispers.

With each passing year, Charmzy's heart began to ache with

profound sadness. The only resolution of this sadness, he believed, was that he was not following his true path, that of the Hemlock Rainbow.

Charmzy felt a strong sense of obligation as he grew older. While he witnessed the world evolving around him, he couldn't shake the feeling of missing out on experiences beyond Dalkey. Despite this, he knew he had to stay to take care of his mother and aging grandmother, Lucy.

Charmzy continued with his school studies and, on weekends, did odd jobs in Dalkey to earn extra income, as his grandmother had grown weak and unable to work.

One afternoon Charmzy was in the kitchen preparing a warm bowl of soup for Lucy. She had been feeling under the weather lately, and he wanted to do something to help her feel better. As he carried the bowl upstairs to her bedroom, he felt a sense of warmth in his heart. He loved his grandmother dearly and was glad to be able to do something to help her.

"Grandmother, I have some warm butternut soup for you." There was no response.

As Charmzy entered the bedroom, he saw his grandmother lying motionless on the bed, her chest still and her eyes closed. The bowl slipped from his trembling hands and shattered on the ground. Lucy's skin was a pale purple. He grabbed her limp, motionless hand. It was cold and lifeless.

Charmzy heard his mother rush up the steps into the bedroom at the sound of shattering glass. He stood there with his face contorted in grief. The room was soon filled with the sound of Charmzy's sobs as Nadella tried to console him, but nothing could take away the pain he felt in his heart.

In the days that followed his grandmother's burial, Charmzy was overwhelmed by memories of laughter and love. However, these memories were now mixed with sadness and loss.

Chapter Three
Destiny Awaits

As the years passed, Charmzy clung to his hopes and childhood dreams, daring to believe in the extraordinary Hemlock Rainbow and its fortunes.

Charmzy was eighteen, transformed into a young man whose heart still beat to the rhythm of childhood wonder. The tales of gold over the rainbow had not been forgotten, but a large part of his very being refused to let go of the stories of gold over the rainbow in the Woods of Hemlock.

The thoughts of the Woods of Hemlock were constantly in Charmzy's mind. Yet, his need to provide for his mother, Nadella, was at the center of his reason not to venture away, and so he continued to work tirelessly as a cobbler in his small village of Dalkey to help support her.

He sat hunched over his workbench, the gentle tapping of his hammer echoing through the quiet room. His calloused hands expertly weaved the laces in and out of the worn leather, a skill he had learned from his beloved grandmother, Lucy. However, his conviction that there was more to life than just the mundane routine of his work grew stronger with each passing day.

Nadella worked on a farm to keep a roof over Charmzy's head, and when Lucy passed away, his mother had to take on odd jobs in the village to replace the income Lucy made as a cobbler. Now that Charmzy had turned eighteen and taken his grandmother's place at the Cobbler's Den, his mother worked only early mornings at the Merchant's Farm.

At the start of her workday, Nadella walked past a pasture where the cows, almost lifeless, stood near a broken fence. The fields were brown and patchy, and once vibrant grass had been reduced to dry tufts that clung to life. The cows mooed weakly because their milk production had fallen off yet again. Nadella sat on a stool with her pail underneath one of the cows. "Please, Margaret, give me some milk so I can get paid for milking. I can't bring droplets to Mr. Merchant."

Just then, a young boy, Liam, arrived with a sack of grain. Nadella watched him lift the heavy sack over a wooden trough. Then she released Margaret, saying, "Okay girl, you go and eat. We will try again tomorrow." She sighed.

As Nadella stood up from her stool, she said, "Careful, Liam." She stepped forward to help him balance the sack. "We can't waste even a handful."

"I know," the boy muttered, his hands smudged with dirt. With Nadella's help, Liam managed to pour the grain in, though some of it spilled onto the ground. The cows crowded around the spilled grains, their long tongues collecting every kernel.

"They don't like the grain as much as the grass," Liam said. Nadella nodded as she looked out onto the empty stretch of pasture. The darkness that shrouded Dalkey had stolen the sun's warmth, leaving the farms barren. Nearly every day, a villager would arrive at the farm with a thin cow in tow because its milk production had dwindled and its owner could no longer afford the grain to nourish it.

Nadella headed over to Mr. Merchant's store. As she entered through a back door, she heard Mr. Merchant talking to a customer in the front of the store. "Good morning, Mr. Garen. What can I help you with?" he asked. Nadella came up and stood beside Mr. Merchant at the counter. Mr. Garen's face was grim.

"Listen, Mr. Merchant, my family barely has enough grain to last the week, and our Daisy won't survive the winter on what we have at home," Mr. Garen said with a heavy heart. "I brought Daisy along. I would like to sell her to you." Mr. Merchant glanced at Nadella with a look of uncertainty.

"Mr. Garen, I don't believe . . ." he began.

Nadella interrupted. "Why, Garen, I may have some grain at home I can spare for your family and Daisy. Keep Daisy and come back tomorrow morning. I'll have a small sack ready for you." Nadella looked at Garen with a wide smile.

"Nadella, I can't take from you and Charmzy," Garen said.

"Mr. Garen, Charmzy and I are doing well. He works full-time at the Cobbler's Den, and we have plenty to spare."

Standing in line behind Mr. Garen was a young girl holding onto wilted carrots. Her mother was still rummaging through the produce boxes. When she arrived at her daughter's side, the woman had a few potatoes in her hands. The girl, her eyes wide with fear, turned to her mother. "Will we starve, Mama?" she asked softly.

The mother knelt down and smiled. "No, my love. We'll find a way—we always do."

Mr. Garen turned back to Nadella, no longer hesitant. "Thank you, Nadella. I will return tomorrow morning." And then he rushed out of the store's swinging door.

Mr. Merchant spoke to Nadella in a low, soft tone. "I know you mean well, but you must not be the savior of everyone that walks through this door."

She nodded. "I understand." Mr. Merchant made his way to the back of the store as Nadella rang up the charges for the mother and her daughter.

The mother looked into Nadella's eyes as her daughter placed their vegetables on the countertop. "It seems the farms are producing less and less these days with that shadow hanging over us," the woman said.

Nadella stared out a side window at a field that had once been green and thriving. Now it was lifeless under a dull, gray sky. The darkness that hung over Dalkey was more than just the absence of light—it was palpable. All the villagers noticed the progression over the years. It felt like a dark force was draining warmth from the earth.

Nadella then turned to face the woman and her daughter. "I have no doubt that the Hemlock Rainbow will shine down on us soon and wash away the gray skies." The girl's eyes lit up at Nadella's words.

"I would love to see the rainbow," the girl said. The mother grabbed her daughter's hand, then looked at Nadella. "I hope that rainbow will arrive soon," she said with a hint of desperation in her voice. Then she turned and walked out.

Nadella began to close up shop. She locked the door and hung her apron behind it. It was time for her to head home to prepare dinner for her and Charmzy.

As she walked through the city center, she saw villagers haggling over withered vegetables and half-full sacks of grain. An elderly man in tattered boots pleaded with a merchant to accept a few coins for a loaf of bread. Nadella thought about how things had gotten so much worse in Dalkey in just the last few months. Crops were dying and villagers scraped the bottom of barrels for an ounce of grain to feed their families.

Around the same time, Charmzy was starting for home after his long hours at work. His spirit, though, was light as he imagined the endless possibilities that the Woods of Hemlock could hold—a hidden fortune, a trove of shimmering gold. But it was not for greed. Charmzy was driven by a deep sense of compassion to use the wealth to assist his struggling mother and the impoverished people of his village.

Despite the promise to his grandmother, Charmzy couldn't shake off the words of the men in the tavern about the gold of the rainbow and the angel. Nor could he forget those Irishmen who had left behind a silence that echoed in their absence to this day. A statue was carved in their image at the town center to honor their bravery. Whenever Charmzy would cross the path of the statue, he would pause, reflecting on the scene he witnessed that night in the tavern with those Irishmen as a young child.

The memory of the seven Irishmen, now immortalized in stone at the town center, weighed on him. Each time he passed their statue, he would pause and reflect on the fateful night in the tavern when they set out, never to return.

One evening, after a long day's work, Charmzy returned home, where Nadella had prepared a hearty dinner. She knew her son well enough to understand the restlessness in his eyes. It was the same longing his father once carried.

"How was your day at the Cobbler's Den? Anything new to share?" she asked, setting a plate in front of him.

Charmzy smiled and responded, "Mr. Murphy delivered a beautiful piece of red leather. He asked me to make a special high heel for Mrs. Murphy as her Valentine's gift."

"Oh, Mr. Murphy is a captivating man," Nadella remarked wistfully, her gaze drifting out the window. "Mrs. Murphy is lucky to have such a husband."

He watched his mother with a mix of admiration and longing. He wished she could experience a love like the Murphys'. His father's absence had left a void that no one could fill.

Charmzy was only three when his father, Finn, passed away suddenly from a heart attack. That loss left a deep emptiness inside him, a longing for the guidance only a father could provide.

His grandmother rarely spoke of Finn, avoiding Charmzy's persistent questions. "It's too painful," she said.

From time to time, though, she would take Charmzy to the river where Finn used to fish, and they would toss flowers into the water. In those moments, Lucy would share fragments of stories about Finn—his favorite songs, his love for the river. These moments were bittersweet for Charmzy, offering him glimpses into his father's life while reminding him of the profound loss he felt.

Occasionally, fleeting memories surfaced in his mind. One was of his father opening a satchel to reveal something to him, though Charmzy could never remember what it was.

Another memory would flash—his father whispering in his ear, but the words were always elusive. Charmzy liked to imagine they were words of love meant just for him.

After dinner, Charmzy wished his mother goodnight, kissed her forehead, and retreated to his bedroom. As sleep overtook him, a dream enveloped him—it was of an angel cloaked in gold and emeralds whispering, "Come, Charmzy, I await your presence."

Each night, the dream grew more vivid. The pull toward the Woods of Hemlock became impossible to ignore, and Charmzy knew that his fate was somehow tied to it. The angel was waiting for him. Charmzy would awaken suddenly, gasping for air, wondering if it was all a dream or if the angel had appeared in his bedroom.

The dream used to occur only once in a while, but when Charmzy turned eighteen, it became more vivid and intense and happened every night. He knew deep inside that his fate was tied to the Woods of Hemlock which held a secret only he could unravel. The angel was telling Charmzy to come to her, but why him?

He awoke the next day knowing that he had a bigger purpose in life than staying in Dalkey and caring for Nadella. He was somehow connected to the Woods of Hemlock.

As the sun painted the sky in shades of rose and gold, Charmzy sat with a breakfast plate before him. Nadella stood in the kitchen, gazing out the window.

"Mother?" Charmzy whispered.

Nadella turned to face him. Her eyes were frozen with fear. "Yes, my sweetness?" she responded. Charmzy felt a piercing in his heart. "Shhhh!" Nadella whispered as she lifted her finger to his lips. "I know you must go. I understand."

Nadella turned and walked down the corridor. She retrieved a duffel bag she had prepared for her son's departure. Her gaze held him with a mix of pride and apprehension as she handed him the bag. Charmzy stood stunned at his mother's great understanding. If it had been his grandmother standing there, she surely would have scolded Charmzy for even the slightest thought of leaving. The weight of Nadella's love and fear hung heavy in the air.

"May the angels guide you back home safely," Nadella said, a prayer woven into her words.

Then she walked over to her credenza and pulled out a satchel. Inside lay a glistening four-leaf clover bigger than Charmzy's two hands and greener than the hat on top of his red hair. In the center of the clover was a bright bud with the shape and sparkle of a diamond.

Nadella spoke softly, "It was your father's most treasured item that he traveled with, and now it is yours. He would want you to have it."

Charmzy was intrigued by the beautiful object, but he told her he could not quite figure out what it was for.

Nadella smiled. "Your father called it a compass—a rare four-leaf compass that could guide him wherever he needed to go. He said that it brought him good luck on his journeys."

She paused, then continued, "Your father kept many secrets, Charmzy. He never told me much about his life before our marriage or why he had to travel to the Woods of Hemlock, but he often left for days, always taking this clover with him. I never knew where he went or what he was doing, but he said I shouldn't ask for protection. It was the same with your grandfather, Ciaran, until one day, he didn't return home to your Grandma Lucy." Charmzy listened intently, feeling the weight of his father's legacy pressing down on him.

Charmzy's eyes widened, "My father traveled to the Woods of Hemlock?" he asked.

"Yes, Charmzy, he did. And so did your grandfather. Ciaran often ventured into the Hemlock Woods," Nadella continued. "The last time your father left, he was gone for weeks. Your grandmother and I gathered a group of villagers and set out to find him. As we ventured deeper, time seemed to warp. One moment we were on a familiar path, the next we were somewhere . . . different—a place that shouldn't exist. The trees twisted unnaturally, the sky dimmed to a strange twilight, and suddenly, we stood before a clearing where a tree shaped like an angel loomed."

"Hemlock Circle?" Charmzy asked. "Why, that must have been Hemlock Circle!"

"I'm sorry, Charmzy, I don't know what that means," she replied.

"Never mind, please carry on. I want to know what happened to my father," Charmzy said.

"Yes, of course, my dear. So suddenly, there was this sudden transition of time and space which was jarring. We became very disoriented, as though the woods had bent the laws of time and space to transport us to this circle. Then, in the center of that circle, bathed in an eerie golden light, lay your father's body." Nadella began to weep. Charmzy grabbed his mother and wrapped his arms around her.

She continued, "Your father's body was still, his face serene as though he had simply fallen asleep. Upon his chest rested the four-leaf clover, its vibrant green glowing faintly in the twilight. It appeared to us that your father had succumbed to a heart attack. His hand was still clutching his chest."

As she stroked his face, Nadella stood back and said, "This is why your Grandma Lucy spoke against you searching for the Hemlock Rainbow. She lost Grandpa Ciaran and then her son, your father, Finn, to the Woods of Hemlock. She and I wanted to protect you from the same fate. But now I can see it's your destiny, and I accept it."

Charmzy looked down and examined the four-leaf clover more closely. He noticed that each point of the diamond shape had a letter indicating north, south, east, and west. With a deep breath, he placed the clover into his bag and hugged his mother tightly, then gave her a final embrace and a promise to return.

Charmzy embarked on his journey with a heart filled with hope and determination and guided by the stories of the past as well as the dreams that now served as his compass. As he turned, he caught sight of Nadella standing in the doorway, her hand raised in a silent, loving farewell.

He gazed over the village, observing men stepping out of their homes to begin their workday, their lives unchanged.

His gaze lingered on the statue in the town center—a tribute to the lost Irishmen and a silent warning of the dangers ahead. But he steadied himself with the thought that he would be fine. The Woods of Hemlock opened up to a realm of mystery, peril, and the promise of answers that had long evaded his family. As he ventured deeper into the forest's shadows, his spirit burned like a torch in the dark, leading him toward his destiny.

CRUMBZY and RALSKY

Chapter Four
Whispers of the Gnomes

arkness and secrets unfolded within the heart of the Woods of Hemlock. The trees stood as towering watchmen, their immense trunks brushing the skies at over three hundred feet, their girth expanding to encircle a hundred feet. The air was damp and chilled and the atmosphere heavy with mystery lurking amidst the shadows.

Hours had passed, and Charmzy began searching for a spot to rest before the sun disappeared and the night took over. As he scouted for a place to settle in, he realized the sun had slipped below the horizon. Instead, soft pale moonlight cast an ethereal glow upon the forest floor. He paused, "This tree looks perfect." He found a hollow in a colossal tree trunk to prop his back on, finally taking a break from his journey to unwrap his salted meat and apple.

Nestling his backpack against the trunk, he fashioned a makeshift pillow and arranged his blankets, surrendering to the night's embrace as it descended upon him. The woods were silent. Not even one nocturnal creature was heard. The only things that seemed to be alive in the woods were the chirping of crickets and the creaking or snapping of branches as the wind blew through them. There were no whistles of nightbirds or hoots from owls, only darkness with a glisten of moonlight through the heavy fog. Wrapped in a fleece blanket, Charmzy succumbed to slumber, his senses entwined with the rhythm of the crickets' singing.

A tender voice called out from the realm of dreams, "Charmzy, Chhhhaarmmzzzy." The sound was a whisper that danced upon the night breeze, a summons that stirred the depths of his subconscious. Slowly, his eyes fluttered open, and before him stood a vision bathed in moonlight—a young woman with hair aflame in hues of red and eyes that shimmered like precious emeralds. Her smile was a radiant dawn and her presence otherworldly.

"At last, you have come," she declared, her voice a gentle caress upon the night air. Charmzy's astonishment was palpable. "Who are you?" he asked, his voice awash with wonder.

"I am Christel, the Angel of the Celestial Realm," she replied. Her eyes locked with his in a profound connection. With a dazzling smile, she continued, "You, Charmzy, are the chosen one."

His words tumbled out, his speech a mix of surprise and disbelief. "The cho-cho-chosen one?" he stuttered, struggling to comprehend the enormity of the moment.

Unbeknownst to Charmzy, he was not alone in the woods. Beneath the canopy, hidden from his sight, two figures watched, Crumbzy and Ralsky, a pair of gnomes. Crumbzy had a chubby face that seemed to have a perpetual grin and a cheerful air about him despite his clumsiness. His ruddy complexion, bright blue eyes, and rounded face gave him a boyish look, as did his blue pointed hat. His short, stout frame carried an air of mischief, and his round belly jiggled slightly with every movement. His clothes, dusty from their travels, consisted of a bright blue cone hat and a beige tunic with a red vest.

Ralsky, on the other hand, was leaner and more serious. His skin was darker and weathered, and he had tousled brown hair and light facial hair. His narrow eyes in a piercing blue seemed to miss nothing. A long, pointed nose gave him an angular appearance, and his dark green vest blended seamlessly with the shadows of the forest. Ralsky moved with precision, his demeanor always calculating and, unlike his cousin, his clothing was practical and unadorned, perfect for blending into the forest underbrush.

A chuckle escaped Crumbzy's lips. "I can't believe this. You must check out this leprechaun, Ralsky! Ha! Ha!" Ralsky's blue eyes darkened, his expression turning severe as he fixed his gaze on Charmzy.

"Believe what?" he inquired, his voice holding a hint of skepticism.

"Listen to what he is saying in his sleep," Crumbzy teased. Ralsky's sharp nose flared as his irritation became palpable.

"Don't you hear him talking in his sleep?" Crumbzy chuckled. Ralsky looked at the leprechaun and, with deep focus, began to listen to what he was saying in his sleep.

As Charmzy continued his dreamlike exchange with Angel Christel, Ralsky's mind whirred, thinking back to the time when the gnomes had once been involved in the ancient battles of the Hemlock Rainbow.

Charmzy's voice echoed in his slumber, "The chosen one, but how is that possible?" he questioned the Angel.

Ralsky's ears perked up at the words, "Chosen one." Ralsky turned to face his cousin Crumbzy to confirm he had heard the same words. The two gnomes looked at one another in surprise, then they both turned their heads back towards Charmzy in his sleep.

Angel Christel's reply came as a whisper: "I must not tell you everything right now. Come to Hemlock Circle. I await your presence."

Charmzy's desperation resonated even in sleep. "Angel! Angel Christel! Don't leave!"

Awakening with a jolt, Charmzy found himself in a frenzy. The realization that he had been chosen electrified his senses. He was no longer a passive observer from his youth in the tavern but a participant in a tale of gold over the rainbow. The sun shone as he rose quickly from the forest floor. He brushed off the remnants of slumber, shaking his head, and spoke with conviction: "I must hurry along to Hemlock Circle, for I am the chosen one, and the riches await me."

The gnomes continued to watch and listen from their hidden spot. Ralsky whispered to his cousin Crumbzy. "You see, he is the chosen one. We must stay close and follow him to the rainbow." Crumbzy nodded.

Charmzy's heart brimmed with a mix of joy and doubt. Could all his hopes and dreams indeed be coming to fruition? As he sprang up, preparing his bag to continue his journey, he began to sing despite his disbelief that he could be the chosen one.

I am the chosen one,
yes, I am.

It was told to me.
Dancing with glee,
over the rainbow,
to the gold I will flee.
For I am the chosen one, indeed!
Through the woods,
where the wild winds blow,
it is time to go!
So, if you see a rainbow
stretching far and wide,
remember the leprechaun
following his star,
for I am the chosen one
on a quest so bold,
and I will capture the gold!

Ralsky, hiding behind a towering tree, spat in disbelief. "This repulsive song is giving me a stomachache. Can you believe this Crumbzy, that this pesky leprechaun is the chosen one?" he muttered as he rubbed his stomach.

Crumbzy, ever the playful one, danced along to the beat of Charmzy's song. "Indeed!" he chimed in, his round belly jiggling with each bounce.

Ralsky's face turned beet red, irritation brewing in his chest. "Crumbzy, don't be a fool! This is our land. We won't let a leprechaun take what belongs to us. It's our gold!"

Crumbzy immediately stopped the dancing and stood up straight with a serious look. "Why, yes, Ralsky, you are right. This is our land. How dare he try to steal our rainbow."

Ralsky looked at Crumbzy with an eyeroll. "Listen here," he said, "I have got the perfect plan," Ralsky had a devilish grin and his sharp nose twitched in excitement. Crumbzy bounced on his heels, his chubby face lighting up in excitement.

"Tell me, tell me!"

"We will let him lead us right to the rainbow," Ralsky whispered, "and once he unlocks the passage, we will shove him aside and claim the gold ourselves!"

Laughter rumbled from Ralsky's belly. Crumbzy nodded eagerly and clapped his hands. "Ha! Brilliant plan, Ralsky! We'll be rich beyond our wildest dreams." Ralsky grabbed his cousin's hands to stop him from clapping and said, "We must be quiet now. We cannot let him know we are following him."

Crumbzy stood up straight and placed his index finger over his lips to signal "shhh," then mimed zipping his lips closed. Ralsky gave a thumbs-up hand motion.

The two gnomes, driven by greed, followed Charmzy through the woods. Stealthily, they darted behind bushes and rocks, their tiny frames easily hidden in the shadows. But as they crept a few meters behind, a sharp snap rang out, freezing them in their tracks. Then, they ducked behind a boulder.

Charmzy spotted a blue robin clutching a twig in its beak. The bird flew away, leaving him to wonder if it was a sign of good luck.

"Just a bird," he murmured, though unease still prickled at the back of his mind. From their hiding spot, Crumbzy grinned and his rosy cheeks glowed with excitement. "I know! We'll befriend the leprechaun," Crumbzy said. But Ralsky sneered. "Never!"

Crumbzy insisted. "Listen, we won't really be his friend. We'll offer help, let him trust us, and strike when he least expects it." Ralsky considered this, his sharp eyes narrowing. "Yes . . . yes, that could work. We'll earn his trust, then take everything when the time is right." He chuckled, patting his cousin's head. "I guess there's a brain in there after all. Ha!"

Crumbzy cupped his mouth to stifle a giggle. "Shall we begin with our anthem?" he asked.

"Why yes, a fitting way to greet our new friend," Ralsky said.

The clanging of tin cups echoed through the woods as the gnomes launched into their rowdy anthem:

We are the Hemlock gnomes, we roam.
No strangers here, we guard our home!
Thieves beware, treasure's our claim.
Try to steal, and you'll rue the name!

Charmzy recognized the song immediately. He turned to face the two gnomes who were now stumbling toward him, tin cups in hand, laughing and exchanging jokes.

"Well, well, what do we have here?" Ralsky asked with a grin.

Crumbzy added, "A little leprechaun in our woods?"

Charmzy straightened. "I know your kind. You're the gnomes who sing about protecting the Woods of Hemlock. I want no trouble."

Already smitten with the idea of playing the friendly gnome, Crumbzy grinned widely. "No trouble at all! We just wanted to see what brings you here. These woods can be dangerous, especially after dark."

Charmzy's eyes narrowed. "I'm just taking a stroll, if you don't mind."

Ralsky snickered. "A stroll, eh? Brave choice. Most don't stroll into Hemlock Woods unless they're looking for something . . . or running from something."

Crumbzy nodded eagerly. "Or someone! So, which is it, friend?"

"We are not friends! Now go along and leave me alone!" Charmzy snapped.

"Oh, but we think you might need some help." Ralsky's eyes gleamed. "A little bird told us you're after something . . . special. Something at the end of a rainbow, perhaps?"

Charmzy's heart raced, but he kept his voice steady. "That's nonsense."

Ralsky leaned in. "Is it? Because we know the truth. You're after the Hemlock Rainbow, aren't you?"

Crumbzy added, "Don't be shy. The Hemlock Rainbow isn't just a myth. But it's guarded—by dark forces. Winfred, the evil warlock, and his twin sister, Madison, have cast spells to protect it. You'll need more than luck to survive."

Charmzy's defiance wavered. "What are you saying?"

Ralsky's expression darkened as his voice took on a grim tone. "They guard the rainbow, and anyone who dares approach it is cursed. Many have died trying. I was there, at the battle for the Hemlock Rainbow. Madison and Winfred, once kind and beloved by all the creatures and nature, crossed the rainbow. But they were forever changed when they returned—twisted by a power beyond their control. They unleashed their newfound magic, dark and unrelenting, turning this once vibrant forest from lush greenery to barren, lifeless brown, just like the cold, empty void in their hearts."

Crumbzy's voice dropped, more serious than ever. "We buried those who fell ourselves. We understand the danger—and the stakes. But we can help you . . . if you let us. All we ask is a share of the gold."

Charmzy weighed his options carefully. Though he didn't trust the gnomes fully, their words rang with a grim truth. "Fine," he said at last. "But let's be clear—forty percent for the two of you, sixty for me. No more."

Ralsky's nostrils flared. "Sixty-forty? For the two of us? No, no, no. We want sixty."

Charmzy shook his head. "Forty-sixty, or I go alone."

Crumbzy, eager to please, nodded quickly. "I . . . I think that's fair. We need you, leprechaun."

Charmzy's brows furrowed in a questionable stare. "What do you mean you need me?"

Ralsky's eyes widened, and he shot Crumbzy a look of disbelief. Crumbzy answered, "Well, you know the tales of the rainbow always included a leprechaun in the mix. Perhaps it's true that we need the help of a leprechaun."

Ralsky looked with pleasure at his cousin's response, yet his face became pale as he realized the truth: without Charmzy—the chosen one—their chances of finding the gold were slim to none. With his jaw clenched, Ralsky reluctantly extended a hand. "Alright, Lep. Forty-sixty it is, but not a coin less!"

"It's Charmzy, not Lep," he replied, hesitating before taking his hand. "Deal. But one trick and your portion of the gold is gone!"

"Deal," Ralsky muttered through gritted teeth.

Crumbzy was eager to seal the pact and blurted out, "Let the journey begin!" His enthusiasm was almost childlike, a stark contrast to the gravity of their agreement.

The three of them placed their hands together, one on top of the other—a gesture of unity, however fragile it might have been. Charmzy watched Ralsky closely, knowing their trust would remain a tenuous thread.

And so, their pact was sealed, bound not just by the promise of wealth but by a delicate alliance that could shatter at any moment. Charmzy, Ralsky, and Crumbzy began their journey toward the Circle of Hemlock, unaware of the dark forces stirring far above Black Rock Mountain. High in the sky, concealed in the shadows of Black Rock Castle, a lurking evil awaited, watching their every move with sinister intent.

Chapter Five
Secrets Unveiled

The air inside Winfred's lair crackled with a deep, unnatural energy. Shadows clung to the ancient stone walls like living things, writhing and twitching as if drawn to the power of the crystal ball glowing between Winfred's clawed fingers. The warlock's ebony eyes gleamed as he peered into the swirling depths of the orb, his expression sharp with suspicion.

"Chelsea," he muttered, not bothering to glance at the red-tailed eagle perched silently by his side. "Look."

The fog in the crystal cleared, revealing three small figures—two gnomes and a leprechaun—creeping through the dark woods of Hemlock. Winfred's lips twisted into a wicked smile.

"Another foolish leprechaun in my woods and gnomes crawling from under their rocks?" His voice dropped, leaving a chilling silence. "They dare trespass on my lands . . . after my treasures."

Chelsea tilted her head, her beady eyes glowing with an eerie light. Her voice didn't echo when she spoke. It slithered into Winfred's mind like an icy whisper. "Shall I summon the forest? The trees will watch them and hear every secret they breathe."

A smile spread across Winfred's face. "Yes. But remind the trees of who rules these woods! It is I, and if they refuse my command, I'll reduce them to ash with a flick of my staff."

"As you wish, Master." Chelsea launched herself into the night without a sound, disappearing into the oppressive canopy of the Woods of Hemlock. The entire forest seemed to shudder when her wings cut through the air.

Far below, Charmzy, Crumbzy, and Ralsky trudged through the twisted, gnarled roots of Hemlock. The air was stifling, heavy with decay and damp earth.

"What is it about this place that makes my skin crawl?" Crumbzy muttered, his voice tight with unease.

Before anyone could answer, a deafening screech ripped through the silence. The noise crashed over them like a physical force, sending them sprawling to the ground. Charmzy clutched his ears, his heart pounding wildly.

"MAKE IT STOP!" Crumbzy screamed, but the sound drowned out his words. It was a screech like a thousand voices crying out in pain, a scream that rattled deep in their bones. Then, as suddenly as it started, it stopped. The silence was thick, suffocating. They scrambled to their feet, gasping for breath, their eyes darting around the oppressive darkness.

"Someone's watching us," Ralsky growled, eyes narrowing.

Charmzy wiped the sweat from his brow, his heart still racing. "Whatever that was, it's not a normal bird."

Chelsea soared high above, her screeches sending commands to the trees and all living things below, instructing them to follow the leprechaun and his companions—and to relay any news of their activities to Black Rock Castle. She darted back to the castle and through the open window. Her eyes flashed as she landed on Winfred's shoulder.

"The forest suspects something, but they know nothing, Master," Chelsea murmured.

Winfred let out a low, sinister chuckle. "Let them scurry. They're gnats before a storm. But I want to know what they're after. Leprechauns are tricksters, every one of them. And I don't take chances."

His eyes glinted as he muttered an incantation, the orb pulsing with a dull, sickly light. The trees in the forest shuddered unnaturally, listening, obeying.

"Shall I summon your sister?" Chelsea asked, her voice icy.

Winfred's smile faded instantly. "No. Not yet. Madison is for . . . later. I don't need her meddling unless this turns into something more than a little hocus-pocus." His long fingers made circles around the orb, and as he and Chelsea peered at the three men, a familiar sensation of hunger and fatigue prompted Crumbzy to suggest a break from the journey. "Ralsky, I'm hungry and tired. Let's rest a bit."

Winfred watched Crumbzy's hands trace circles over his stomach. He sighed and turned to Chelsea. "I'm getting bored with this. Let's grab some lunch."

"Yes, Master," she responded. Then, Winfred and Chelsea left the room, strolling down the corridors of the castle as they chatted about the most tempting dishes they could indulge in.

Crumbzy grumbled for the second time. "Ralsky, I'm hungry and tired. Let's rest a bit."

"Do not disturb my thoughts, Crumbzy. I'm thinking," Ralsky responded curtly.

Crumbzy whispered, "Thinking about what?"

Ralsky's voice held an air of authority. "The purpose of that four-leaf clover in Charmzy's backpack." The gnomes were fascinated by its beauty. It shimmered and sparkled in the sunlight, sticking halfway out of the back pocket of Charmzy's sack.

"Why not just ask him?" Crumbzy responded.

Mimicking Crumbzy in a mocking tone, Ralsky repeated, "Well, why don't you just ask him?"

Crumbzy, undeterred, approached Charmzy by his side as they continued walking the path and asked, "Hey there, Lep, whatcha got in that satchel?"

Charmzy turned to Crumbzy, stopped briefly, and replied, "I have water and bread."

"Excellent, because I'm starving and ready for a break," Crumbzy said with relief. Charmzy reached down for the food in his bag.

Ralsky chimed in and clarified, nudging Crumbzy's side with his elbow, "No, he means, what is that shiny four-leaf clover you got in your bag?"

"Ouch! That hurt, Ralsky!" Crumbzy yelped, rubbing his side.

"I'll be asking the questions," Ralsky told Crumbzy.

Charmzy looked puzzled as he remembered that he had the four-leaf clover. He retrieved it from his satchel and displayed it to the gnomes in both palms. Ralsky and Crumbzy gazed upon it, captivated by its beauty. "What is it?" asked Crumbzy.

"I'm not entirely sure," Charmzy explained, as he held the delicate object in his hand and gazed at it wistfully.

"It was my father's. He took it with him on all his travels. My mother kept it for me until I journeyed away from home. It's the only thing I have left from him," he said sadly. "I believe this four-leaf clover is a compass. Perhaps it will guide me to the Hemlock Circle, but I don't know." Charmzy shrugged.

Crumbzy continued to gaze upon the four-leaf clover. "May I hold it?" he asked, his eagerness palpable.

Charmzy nodded and handed him the clover but not before warning him to be careful. "It's a precious family heirloom. Please be very careful," he said. His eyes fixed on Crumbzy's hand as he passed him the clover. Crumbzy was trembling with excitement. As the clover landed in his hand, its weight was unexpected for its rather small size. It slipped from between Crumbzy's palms and tumbled, hitting the ground.

Crumbzy tried to catch it in a whirl of panic but couldn't move fast enough. It rattled and clanked as it hit the ground and bumped up against a few rocks before stopping. Charmzy, Ralsky, and Crumbzy watched in shock, their attention locked on the fallen clover.

Suddenly, a soft, childish voice spoke up. "That hurt!"

Perplexed, they exchanged glances and looked around to see who it might be. "Who said that?" Ralsky questioned.

"Down here!" the voice replied. Their gazes returned to the four-leaf clover.

Crumbzy stumbled back, wide-eyed, and exclaimed, "Did . . . did that thing just talk?"

Ralsky's skepticism was evident. "Clovers don't talk."

The four-leaf clover introduced itself cheerfully, "Hello, I'm Cloveris." A mix of amazement and disbelief swept over them. Charmzy managed to utter, "It does speak!"

Cloveris' voice was gentle but confident. "Indeed, I do, Charmzy. And you, my keeper, are the one I've been waiting for."

Charmzy looked bewildered. "Keeper? What does that mean?" His mind raced with questions and a knot of anxiety tightened in his chest.

Cloveris' glowing form flickered as if sensing the weight of the confusion Charmzy felt. "I come from a long line of magical four-leaf clovers known as The Clovers. We are the children of the rainbow. I am the last of my kind. When I was just an infant, Angel Christel entrusted me to your father, Finn. I was meant to be his compass to the location of the rainbow. But when his time ended, she put me into a deep slumber, waiting for the chosen one—you—to awaken me and carry on the legacy."

Ralsky and Crumbzy's eyes widened in disbelief as they absorbed Cloveris' words. The two cousins exchanged stunned glances as they struggled to process what they had just heard. All three men were taken aback. The enormity of what Cloveris was saying about four-leaf clovers and his legacy pressed down on Charmzy, making his heart pound.

"Legacy? What does that mean? But how? How is this even possible? I'm just a leprechaun," he stammered. His voice trembled and his breath became shallow as the truth unfolded.

The soft glow coming from Cloveris pulsed with sympathy. "Your father, Finn, was the last guardian of the Hemlock Rainbow. He inherited that duty from your grandfather, Ciaran, whose family before him made a sacred pact with Angel Christel and the ethereal beings when my family—the Clovers—were slowly fading from existence. The Clovers were once the front-line protectors of Hemlock Rainbow and kept the balance of the realms. But over time, many Clovers were lost, succumbing to battles with dark magic and the weakening of the natural world. In exchange for safeguarding the natural world and the magical entities of the many other realms, the Cloverborn bloodline was endowed with the power of the Clovers—a rare and potent magic drawn from the heart of the four-leaf clover."

Charmzy listened intently but still felt confused about what this meant. "So, if I'm correct, you are telling me that I have special powers?"

"Yes, that is correct, Charmzy," Cloveris said.

"And that these powers have been passed down to me from my bloodline?" asked Charmzy in hesitant confusion.

"Yes, Charmzy. If I can explain a bit more." Cloveris continued. "You see, this magic is intricately tied to rainbows, nature, spirits, and life. It is the sacred duty of the Cloverborn lineage to protect the power of the Hemlock Rainbow, which holds the key to all rainbows, maintaining peace and keeping nature vibrant while preserving the balance between the human and celestial realms."

"How? How do I find this hidden magic I have within me? And why has it never shown itself before?" Charmzy asked.

"Charmzy, you are now of age to wield your powers. As the Guardian of the Hemlock rainbow, you will be able to unlock your powerful magic soon enough. And with that magic, you will stand against the forces of dark magic," Cloveris said.

Ralsky and Crumbzy stood quietly in awe of the pulsating four-leaf clover, taking in every word.

"The Guardian of the Rainbow," Charmzy repeated, his voice tinged with disbelief. He began pacing around Cloveris, his thoughts racing as he took in the enormity of his heritage. The realization that he was a descendant of the anointed Cloverborn bloodline stirred an anxiety deep in his chest. He wondered to himself, just what did it mean to be connected to such ancient magic?

Charmzy thought of Grandma Lucy's constant warnings and her desperate attempts to shield him from the dangers of Hemlock. Perhaps she had been right all along. First, his grandfather vanished, and then his father had died—supposedly from natural causes. But now, Charmzy couldn't shake the growing suspicion that his father's death wasn't natural at all. Could it have been black magic?

Meanwhile, Ralsky edged closer to his cousin Crumbzy, casting a sidelong glance at Charmzy. Leaning discreetly, he muttered into Crumbzy's ear, "So, the Lep has magic. This could be a problem for us."

Crumbzy, always quick with a response, leaned back and whispered with a grin, "Problem? We're pint-sized powerhouses, Ralsky." Their eyes locked, a shared mischievous glint between them. Both gnomes clamped their lips shut, holding back the urge to burst into laughter in the middle of such a tense moment.

Charmzy turned to Cloveris. "My father never spoke of this, nor did my grandmother." It felt like the world he knew had been turned upside down.

"Or perhaps your father, Finn, did speak to you about this, but you blocked it out." Cloveris suggested it gently. "Let me help you to remember," he said. Then suddenly, a soft beam of light shot from the center of Cloveris' diamond bud, striking Charmzy's forehead. He fell into a state of remembrance.

An image appeared in his mind. He was just a toddler, his father kneeling beside him, whispering in his ear, while Grandma Lucy stood silently in the doorway, watching over them.

"My son, you are the Guardian of Hemlock Rainbow. All its power and treasures are yours to protect. If anything happens to me, you must find the Angel and the rainbow and stand against the Malrend family. Protect life. It's your duty, my son. I love you, Charmzy," his father's voice echoed.

Another image appeared of Finn opening the satchel, showing Charmzy the glowing four-leaf clover. "Charmzy, this is Cloveris. He is in my care and one day he will be your friend. You both are the same age." Then Finn kissed his son's forehead and whispered, "I love you."

The image faded, and Charmzy gasped. "My dreams! The flash images. Now I understand what that whisper was—my father telling me . . ."

"Yes, Charmzy," Cloveris said softly. "Your father, Finn, told you many stories of your lineage when you were young. It's all there in your heart, waiting for you to unlock it and embrace your true purpose as the Guardian of Hemlock Rainbow."

"This is all so much for me to take in. Give me a moment to clear my thoughts," Charmzy said. He continued pacing with sweat dripping from his forehead.

Crumbzy stepped towards Charmzy and placed his hand on his back. "Perhaps it's best to take a seat." He pulled a log towards Charmzy who then sat down with his face in his hands.

"I need to tell you more, Charmzy," Cloveris said.

With a sigh, Charmzy lifted his head from his hands and responded. "Why yes, please continue."

"Your grandfather, Ciaran, and his father before swore an oath to protect the magic of the rainbow from those who would abuse its power. Your father, Finn, upheld that same oath. But the magic within the rainbow is ancient, and though it produces good magic, it can be dangerous at the same time, especially in the hands of the Malrend family . . . Are you following along?" Cloveris asked.

Charmzy stood and grabbed up Cloveris from the ground. "Yes, I'm listening. Please continue," he replied.

"After Ciaran never returned home, the rainbow gradually began to turn indigo and violet, fading all the other colors and creating darkness in Hemlock which was once a vibrant forest. That's when your father was summoned to the rainbow by Angel Christel."

"My father . . . he went to the rainbow?" Charmzy asked, his voice trembling.

"Yes, to investigate what was happening inside. The once-green forest was turning brown. When we arrived, your father unlocked the rainbow and ventured inside, but I could not follow him," Cloveris explained. "At that time, my powers were not fully developed. I was too young and couldn't access the rainbow's magic, no matter how much I tried to draw strength from it. Some ancient magic was at work, blocking the power of the four-leaf clovers. That's how my family became lost and weakened through the ages. It was a powerful black magic that had returned. I believe that Madison and Winfred Malrend gained access to the rainbow's dark magic."

His voice grew soft with sorrow, a sadness that mirrored the weight of his words.

"Why didn't my mother tell me? Why didn't Grandma Lucy?" Charmzy asked, trembling with disbelief.

Cloveris' glow dimmed, reflecting the gravity of the truth. "They never knew, Charmzy. They believed your father had succumbed to an illness, as his body was found just outside the rainbow's reach. They never understood the true nature of his final journey. He went to protect the Hemlock Rainbow from an encroaching darkness—a darkness that has only grown stronger since."

Ralsky chimed in, "Cloveris, this is some heavy news. Maybe dial it back a bit? I think Charmzy needs some breathing room. Give us a moment, will you?" Ralsky handed over the four-leaf clover to Crumbzy who made sure not to drop it this time. Ralsky then gestured for Charmzy to step aside, away from Cloveris.

Once they were out of earshot, Ralsky leaned in and whispered, "Listen here, Lep, we gnomes are here to help you. You don't need this little plant slowing us down. Why don't we toss him aside and go straight for the gold?"

Charmzy's eyes widened as he raised his voice. "Are you out of your mind? Did you not hear a word Cloveris said? I'm his keeper! I'm not going to abandon him like some worthless trinket!"

Ralsky blinked, momentarily taken aback by Charmzy's sharp tone. He narrowed his eyes, his usual smirk faltering.

"Keeper or not, gold's the real prize here, Lep. Don't lose sight of that." He crossed his arms, his voice dropping to a conspiratorial whisper. "Don't let this clover nonsense get in the way of what's waiting at the end of that rainbow. Do you think this 'guardian' business will keep you safe when real danger strikes? We gnomes can handle that. Not some talking plant."

Crumbzy, sensing the rising tension, stepped in to diffuse the situation. "Hold on, Ralsky, let's not get too hasty here." He shot a glance at Charmzy and in a lighter, almost pleading tone, said, "We're all in this together, right? Maybe the clover's got a role to play, and maybe we do too. We can still get the gold, but maybe we can let Charmzy handle the clover thing, right? No need to make enemies when we're on the same side."

Ralsky's lips twisted in frustration, but after a long pause, he gave a begrudging nod. "Fine. But don't say I didn't warn you when things go south." He jabbed a finger in Charmzy's direction. "Just remember, we're not here to play hero. We're here to win."

The weight of his father's sacrifice pressed down on Charmzy, heavier than anything he had ever felt. It was a burden he hadn't even known he carried. Charmzy plucked the clover from Crumbzy's hands and said, "So . . . my father died protecting the rainbow, and now I'm supposed to take his place?"

Cloveris' light pulsated. "Yes, Charmzy."

Charmzy also felt the weight of Ralsky's words pressing on him. He knew deep down that the gnomes' motivations were far from noble. Gold, riches, treasure— it was all they cared about. But now, with Cloveris by his side, Charmzy was no longer just a leprechaun chasing after gold. He had a greater responsibility.

He glanced at Crumbzy who, despite his playful nature, at least seemed open to the possibility of teamwork. But Ralsky's greed was palpable—his eyes gleamed too much when he spoke of gold and Charmzy could sense the undercurrent of betrayal lurking just beneath the surface.

Charmzy stroked Cloveris' leaves as the gnomes looked on. "I'll watch them closely," Cloveris whispered to Charmzy.

"I'll take their help, but I can't fully trust them. Not until they prove they care about more than just the riches," Charmzy told Cloveris. Glancing back at the gnomes, Charmzy forced a tight smile. "I'll keep you by my side, Cloveris," he said, holding the clover firmly against his chest.

As the gnomes continued watching his every move, Charmzy turned to face Crumbzy and Ralsky and said, "We're still a team. Remember—if we reach the rainbow, the real treasure is to protect its magic, not hoard the gold." He then locked eyes with Ralsky and said, "Cross me, and you'll lose more than just your share."

His warning was clear. Ralsky's eyes narrowed, but he nodded, though the tension between them lingered.

Meanwhile, high above, Winfred and Chelsea returned from their full and leisurely lunch. Winfred's laughter echoed through the stone chamber as he again sat before the orb. "Let's see what our little wanderers have been up to while we were away."

Chelsea landed beside him, her talons clicking against the stone. "Do you think they've uncovered anything?" she asked, her voice dripping with intrigue. Winfred's grin widened as he peered into the glowing orb.

"I doubt it," he said, his tone rising with amusement. "But let's have some fun. It's been too long since I've played a good game of cat and mouse." The twisted sound from his dark laugh made the shadows dance.

As the orb flickered to life, revealing the three travelers deep in the

Woods of Hemlock, Winfred raised his staff and muttered an incantation. "Let's see how brave they are when the forest turns against them."

Far below, the trees began to stir. The path that once lay before the trio shifted, twisting into a maze of darkened roots and towering branches. Strange shapes danced in the distance—illusions conjured by Winfred's dark magic. The air grew thick and cold and whispers threaded through the leaves like ghostly fingers. The gnomes looked at one another in fear but continued their journey following the leprechaun deeper into the Woods of Hemlock. The forest itself began to shift. Using his dark magic, Winfred manipulated the landscape, causing the trees to uproot and tumble, paths to veer off into deep ravines, and strange illusions to appear menacingly close. The group was becoming disoriented and seeds of doubt sprung up amongst them.

Suddenly, the trio found themselves trapped in a maze of trees that hadn't been there moments before. The air grew colder and faint whispers filled the forest. Already on edge, the gnomes turned their suspicions toward Charmzy and Cloveris. "This isn't normal," Crumbzy muttered, glancing nervously at the shifting forest. "The trees have changed and the path is different."

Ralsky clenched his fists. "This is no ordinary forest magic. What if you're leading us into a trap?" he snapped at Charmzy.

"I'm doing no such thing. I'm just as confused as you are," Charmzy said, snapping back at Ralsky.

"Maybe that Cloveris of yours is playing us all," Ralsky suggested. Charmzy's brow furrowed as his frustration with the gnomes' suspicions festered. Crumbzy, the more cheerful of the two, began to shift uneasily.

"Yeah, Lep," Crumbzy added, backing away slightly. "What if Ralsky is right? The forest didn't start acting up until your four-leaf clover started talking. How do we know this isn't all part of some trick?"

"Enough!" Charmzy snapped, his voice cutting through the rising doubts. "Cloveris isn't the one playing tricks on us. This is the work of something far darker. We won't leave these woods alive if we don't stick together." He fixed his gaze on the gnomes.

Ralsky's eyes flickered for a moment, but he wasn't ready to fight with Charmzy just yet. Charmzy squared his shoulders, prepared to defend his position, when Coveris' voice broke through the tension, calm yet commanding.

"Charmzy, the time has come to trust in who you are. The power of the Clovers flows through your veins. This is your destiny—to protect the Hemlock Rainbow and everything it guards. But you won't face it alone. I will guide you." The clover's diamond-like bud glowed brighter. Cloveris was a small but fierce beacon of hope against the dark, shifting woods. The warmth of his magic light seeped into Charmzy's skin, anchoring him to his purpose.

Just as the light from Cloveris grew, Winfred's orb flickered twice far away in the castle of Black Rock and then went dark. Immediately, the dark woods shifted away from the three men and they were no longer trapped in the maze.

"What just happened?" Winfred snarled, frustration dripping from his voice. "Just when the cat-and-mouse game was getting interesting." Disappointed, he turned to Chelsea and ordered her to follow up with any new information she might get from the Woods of Hemlock.

"Why yes, my master." Chelsea nodded.

Back in the woods, Charmzy turned to the gnomes, his voice firm and steady. "Things have changed drastically for me. I'm no longer here just for the gold, Ralsky. I'm now here to save something far more valuable, and if you can't see it, you're free to leave."

Charmzy then turned his back on them, daring them to follow or abandon the mission.

For a long, tense moment, the forest held its breath. Then, Ralsky's defiance wavered. The stubborn fire in his eyes dimmed ever so slightly as he watched the twisted trees creep back away.

Crumbzy looked at his cousin, reluctant to speak on his behalf. Ralsky eyed Crumbzy who shook his head in somewhat agreement with Charmzy.

"Please stop," Ralsky told Charmzy. Charmzy turned around and stared at Ralsky, awaiting his response.

"Alright, Lep, we are in till the end," Ralsky said with conviction. His voice was low but confident in his decision. Charmzy nodded, knowing that their fragile truce hung by a thread. He turned around and continued moving forward, knowing that from here on out there was no turning back. Whether the gnomes followed or not, he would see this through.

The woods seemed to close in behind him as if sealing his path forward—and whatever waited at the end of it.

Chapter Six
A Royal Confrontation

Ralsky and Crumbzy exchanged glances. For the first time, something had shifted inside Ralsky. He had seen Charmzy as no more than a means to riches, but as the weight of the revelations settled, he began to question his intentions.

As their stomachs growled, Charmzy glanced at the dipping sun. "Let's stop for a moment," he said, his voice softer than usual. "We've had enough shocks for one day."

They found a quiet spot in the woods where the golden light filtered through the trees. Charmzy rummaged through his satchel, pulling out the last of their provisions. Silence hung between them as they ate, each lost in thought over the newfound gravity of their mission.

Crumbzy was never one to stay silent for long. As soon as he wiped his mouth, he said, "Well, that's a lot to chew on—both the lunch and your whole 'protecting the rainbow' thing, Charmzy."

Ralsky grunted. "A guardian of the Hemlock Rainbow . . . and Finn, Ciaran. You're carrying a lot on those tiny shoulders, Charmzy."

"I am," Charmzy said quietly, his gaze fixed on the fading sun. "But I know what I have to do. I'll finish what my father started. We need to reach Hemlock Circle."

Ralsky stretched and stood. "Then let's get moving before it gets dark."

Crumbzy crouched, his hands pressed to the ground. "Hold up. I feel something." His eyes widened. "It's horses. Fast."

"They're coming right at us," Ralsky muttered, scanning the horizon. He tensed, ready for trouble. "They're not slowing down!"

Charmzy stood, his eyes narrowing. "We need to intercept them. We're low on supplies and horses would get us to Hemlock Circle faster."

The trio stood their ground, dust swirling around their boots as the thundering of hooves grew louder. Before they could react, a brilliant light erupted from Charmzy's backpack, casting an otherworldly glow around them. The ground beneath their feet seemed to hum as a shimmering barrier materialized, its edges flickering with hues of violet and gold. The riders, galloping at full speed, didn't have time to stop. Their horses screamed in panic as they collided with the invisible wall.

Hooves scraped against the dirt and riders were thrown from their saddles. Some flipped over their horses' heads, landing in tangled heaps, while others tumbled sideways, crashing into each other. The clattering of armor filled the air as horses reared, their panicked whinnies echoing through the trees.

The dust settled, revealing a scene of chaos. Several of the riders lay on the ground, groaning, dazed and confused, while others scrambled to their feet, swords drawn, their faces pale with shock.

"What the—?!" one of the soldiers muttered, wide-eyed, stumbling backward as if he had seen a ghost.

Another rider, his face etched with fear, looked to his comrades, his hand trembling as he gripped his sword.

"Magic!" he whispered. "That was magic! I told you these woods are cursed."

A deep, commanding voice boomed from the back of the group. "What has transpired here?"

Charmzy, ever composed, stepped forward, the glowing barrier still shimmering behind him. "Greetings. I am Charmzy, and we seek your assistance. Would you kindly step out of your chariot?"

The towering figure that emerged was King Olaf Thunderbeard. His amber hair, crowned with golden leaves, cascaded down his back like wildfire, his soft hazel eyes, fierce yet calm. He wore a rich crimson tunic with intricately embroidered designs. Olaf's broad chest was protected by a thick bronze armor with engravings of ancient runes. Around his waist he wore a silver chainmail skirt that was well polished and, on his feet, boots plated in gold.

The massively-built man jumped out from his chariot. Two soldiers stood at attention on each side. Despite their confusion, they brandished golden swords and wore silver armor. Their fear was momentarily forgotten in the presence of their king. But the shock lingered in their eyes, and their breathing was still ragged from the unexpected halt.

King Olaf lifted his large muscular arms adorned with golden-studded leather gauntlets above his head. Swiftly, he retrieved a long golden axe with emeralds on the handle from behind him. He twirled it effortlessly in one hand as he strode toward them.

"I'll slice you three little piggies in half!" His voice was calm, but the threat was unmistakable. He brazenly swung it from side to side and twirled it up and down in his hand like a ball as he approached the three men.

"You're not slashing anyone!" Ralsky snapped, stepping forward with his fists clenched, his rage bubbling over. His eyes blazed and his face flushed with anger as he approached the large amber-haired man. Always quick to action, Ralsky widened his stance, ready to defend his friends.

Crumbzy darted in front of Ralsky, blocking his path. "Pardon me, but . . . are you a deity?" His curiosity usually got the better of him, but this time it served as a well-timed distraction.

The King paused, then let out a deep, rumbling laugh. "No, I am no god. I am King Olaf Thunderbeard of Nordheimer, Viking King."

Ralsky snorted, barely suppressing a laugh, but quickly fell silent as the king peered over Crumbzy's shoulder, eyes locked on Ralsky.

"Oh my! A Viking king?" gasped Crumbzy, who promptly knelt and bowed his head. Ralsky nudged his cousin from behind, causing Crumbzy to lurch forward and kiss the king's dazzling shoe. Known for his respectful nature, Crumbzy's actions were genuine, though sometimes clumsy.

The still jittery horses pawed at the ground, their nostrils flaring.

Several soldiers exchanged nervous glances, unsure whether to fight or flee after the display of magic. But King Olaf wasn't so easily scared. His gaze shifted to the barrier faintly flickering behind the three travelers.

"Tell me, little leprechaun," he growled, stepping closer to Charmzy. "Where did that magic come from?" King Olaf's expression darkened. "Why have you halted my horsemen? And what magic stops my army?"

Ralsky widened his stance still more and was about to respond when Charmzy raised his hand, cutting off Ralsky's retort.

"We mean no disrespect. We're on a journey to Hemlock Circle and could use your guidance. Perhaps you might spare some horses and provisions?"

The king narrowed his eyes as he circled them, the axe resting on his shoulder. "Hemlock Circle, you say? I know the way. It's far from where we stand." He stopped, inspecting the faint glow from Charmzy's backpack. "But what interests me more is that magic. The one that stopped my men."

Crumbzy bowed again, this time with more grace. "Your Majesty, we only seek your help to reach our destination." The king ignored him, stepping closer to Charmzy. "Tell me, little leprechaun, where did that magic come from?"

Charmzy stiffened. "I don't know what you're talking about."

"Don't play coy with me." Olaf's voice was a low growl. "I have all the gold I need. But magic? Now, that's a rare thing. I'm more interested in how you summoned that shield." Charmzy held his ground, his voice steady and his eyes serious.

"I don't have magic, Your Majesty. Whatever you saw, I didn't cause it. Either you help us, or we leave right now!"

The king eyed him for a long moment, then erupted in laughter.

"I like you, leprechaun. You've got guts. Here's my offer. Stay at my castle for the night, rest up, and I'll supply you with horses and provisions for your journey to Hemlock Circle in the morning. But know this—I'll be keeping a close eye on you . . . and this magic you claim not to have."

Crumbzy and Ralsky exchanged eager glances. Their eyes darted to the chariot filled with beautiful women and platters of fresh fruit.

"Yes!" Ralsky shouted, his earlier anger forgotten. He leaped into the chariot, his legs crossed and his back reclined. A moment later, he found himself surrounded by a bevy of women rushing to feed him grapes. Crumbzy bowed again to the king, then spun around and dove headfirst into the chariot. The king raised an eyebrow, clearly puzzled by Crumbzy's odd behavior.

Charmzy, ever the diplomat, said, "Thank you, King Thunderbeard. Your hospitality is appreciated."

"Call me King Olaf," he replied, hopping back into his chariot and leading them toward his castle.

As they traveled, Charmzy leaned toward his satchel and whispered, "Hey, Cloveris, that was some impressive magic back there. I will not tell King Olaf it was you."

Cloveris spoke, his voice low and puzzled. "I did not cast any spell, Charmzy. I'm as clueless as you are." Charmzy's brow furrowed.

If Cloveris had not caused it, then where had the magic come from? He glanced at the glowing violet sky and the crimson setting sun casting long shadows over the land. Whatever it was, it felt . . . different. The scenery shifted as the chariot rolled on past towering mountains and dried, cracked lakes that once shimmered with life. Charmzy could almost see the lost beauty of Hemlock. But one question lingered: Was the magic within him? Sitting at the back of the chariot, Charmzy gripped his satchel tightly, his mind buzzing with wonder as the wheels of the chariot rattled over the rough road.

KING OLAF THUNDERBEARD

Chapter Seven
Nordheimer Castle

The freshness of churned earth and the faint scent of burning wood wafted toward the three companions, carried on the evening breeze. In the distance beyond a tree-lined path and dark plumes of smoke rose King Olaf's castle. The promise of warmth and the smell of roasting meat teased the air, hinting at a feast within stone walls as they entered the gates.

The guests marveled at the enormous structure as the chariot arrived at Nordheimer Castle. Tall golden gates stood imposingly against the rugged landscape, emanating an aura of ancient strength and grandeur. On exiting the chariot, the gnomes and the leprechaun followed King Olaf up a path lined with emerald stones, which led to a massive wooden door engraved with a Viking insignia.

The castle doors opened, carrying the scent of burning hearths. Charmzy, with his emerald-green attire and a twinkle in his eye, marveled at the architecture before him. The castle's towering spires reached towards the heavens, a testament to Viking craftsmanship that blended seamlessly with the enchanting surroundings.

The echoes of footsteps on polished stone floors greeted Charmzy and his companions as they entered the grand hall. King Olaf Thunderbeard walked ahead of them to sit on his majestic velvety throne. His presence was as impressive as the castle. King Olaf's eyes, filled with wisdom and strength, locked onto the tiny visitors who stood before his throne.

Suddenly, the room was filled with a high-pitched, almost eerie laughter that seemed to come from nowhere. A tall, slender figure emerged from the shadows in the northern corner of the room dressed in mismatched colors and patterns on his tights and gold slippers. His disheveled hair and crooked hat adorned with golden bells jingled softly as he moved. The man began to dance and, with grace and fluidity, slid effortlessly beside King Olaf's throne.

After a long silence, the slender man finally spoke, his voice still laced with amusement. "Why, hello there, little people!" he exclaimed. "I'm Jack the Jester, but you can call me Jack."

He slowly walked towards the three puny men, his tall figure looming over them. As he approached, he circled them, making them feel even smaller. The men looked up at his thin stature, their faces contorting with frustration and anger. Jester Jack seemed to find their reactions amusing. As Jack looked down at the three men standing before him, a wide grin spread across his face. He laughed, tilted his head back, and twirled around them.

"Well, well, well," he exclaimed, "aren't you three a sore sight to behold?"

With a flick of his wrist, Jack swiped his fingers up and down their shirts, inspecting their clothing with an unpleasant expression on his face. The tension was about to boil over when a voice rumbled through the room.

"Okay, that will be enough, Jack," King Olaf said in his deep, stoic voice. The jester's laughter died down and he stopped twirling. He bowed respectfully to the king and the three little men before retreating to the corner of the room.

"Welcome, my new friends, to Castle Nordheimer!" King Olaf's voice resonated warmly, and the hall filled with staff cheering and welcoming the three men. "Now, let's celebrate our new friendship over a feast. Jack, guide our guests to their respective chambers to freshen up before dining."

With eagerness, Jack the Jester appeared from the corner, extending an open hand towards the entrance of the corridor where he stood. His other hand lay across his lower backside as he said, "After you." He wore a wide open grin as he stared into their eyes.

Hesitantly, the three men moved ahead of Jack while Ralsky shot him a fierce look over his shoulder.

Jack giggled at Ralsky's brutishness and coyly fluttered his lashes.

Ralsky grunted and cleared his throat. He felt unsettled by Jack's flirtatious gesture and quickly turned back to face forward.

Jester Jack led them to three separate chambers as the men entered the dimly lit hallway lined with paintings of Viking kings from ages past. Each chamber was magnificently furnished with an impressive array of art and artifacts as well as bowls of succulent berries. The jester's eyes sparkled with mischief as he reminded them that each chamber had a wardrobe closet containing a change of clothes for them to wear. He stressed the importance of dressing well when dining with King Olaf, a man known for his refined taste and love of extravagance.

Jester Jack's playful tone turned serious as he urged the men to hurry. "The Majesty has an insatiable appetite that starts at the strike of 8 o'clock. He does not like to be kept waiting. His appetite will be at its peak at that time." Then Jack twirled his way down the hallway until he could no longer be seen.

"That is one odd fella," Ralsky said with a chuckle, shaking his head in disbelief.

"Okay, let's hurry along," Charmzy insisted.

Shortly after they had retreated to their chambers, the doors swung open to reveal the three men now dazzling in their new attire. They hurried down the hallway.

"Wait," Charmzy said, "I'll be just a moment." He returned to his chamber to retrieve his satchel. "I can't leave Cloveris behind." They then continued hurrying on their way when suddenly a shout of "Boo!" roared from Jack. He was at the end of the hallway slightly hidden from sight. The three men jumped, startled.

Jack laughed and said snidely, "Impressive! You all clean up well. Follow me to the banquet hall."

A lavish feast in the banquet hall made their empty bellies grumble even louder. Crumbzy's belly was the loudest of them all. The king sat majestically at the head of the table, dressed in his royal robes. Standing behind him, the staff quickly went around the table to pull out seats for the trio. The tantalizing aroma of pheasant, pork ribs, an abundance of side dishes, and various gourmet desserts filled the air, making their mouths water.

With an inviting smile and open arms, King Olaf declared, "Welcome to my grand banquet table. Please, don't be shy to feast until your bellies are brimming with delight."

"Why thank you, your Majesty," Crumbzy replied gleefully. He then leaped from his seat to seize every decadent food item that he could fit onto his plate, his enthusiasm unbridled. Charmzy and Ralsky followed after Charmzy again thanked the king for his great hospitality.

"Let's get down to business, shall we?" King Olaf said. "I'm willing to assist you in your travels to Hemlock Circle. But I must ask again, what kind of magic do you possess that instantly stopped my army? Such power could be beneficial to my kingdom during battles."

"I understand your concerns, Your Majesty," Charmzy said. "Still, I must reiterate that I am unaware of the source of this power. I have nothing to hide." The king sat quietly with one eye raised in suspicion as he ripped the skin from a turkey drumstick with his front teeth.

"Well, you do have something magical. Maybe it was that magical four-leaf clover who put the wall of magic there," Crumbzy mumbled through a mouthful of food.

"Crumbzy, what you are saying is absurd. There is no such thing as a magical four-leaf clover," Ralsky scoffed.

Intrigued and puzzled, King Olaf looked on intrigued and puzzled as Ralsky and Charmzy exchanged glances.

Crumbzy, too absorbed in his meal to notice the glances, continued staring at his plate and said, "Did you forget about Cloveris? Maybe it was him?"

Ralsky stood up and hit the table with his fist, causing the apples to bounce. Crumbzy finally stopped eating to look up from his plate. "Oops, I meant nothing," he said.

"I will be the only one who pounds on my banquet table!" King Olaf clapped his hands, pounding the table as he stood up.

"Now, where is this Cloveris? Is he in your chamber? Guards, go to their chambers at once and tell Cloveris to come out. How did this fellow get past me? Is he another clever little leprechaun?" the king questioned.

The three men sat motionless, their minds racing with uncertainty as they pondered what would transpire once the guards returned empty-handed from searching the chambers. All was silent except for the sound of the guards' boots as they marched away.

King Olaf's face turned red as he shouted with fury, spewing bits of turkey from his mouth. "Do you take me for a fool? I offer you a safe haven of food and rest, and what do I receive in return but deceit and lies!"

"I found nobody in their chambers, Your Majesty," announced the guard with his sword drawn. The king approached Crumbzy with his mighty axe drawn from his back. The axe, shining with emeralds on the handle, caused Crumbzy to quake. The king came from behind Crumbzy with the axe in his hand and, bending down to his ear, instructed him to call out for Cloveris.

"Cloveris, dear Cloveris, please come out, come out wherever you are," Crumbzy said, his voice sounding shaky and worried.

Charmzy remained calm as he glanced at Cloveris resting in his satchel. Something about the clover had been nagging at Charmzy throughout the evening, a feeling of unease as if there was much more to Cloveris than he knew about. Charmzy picked up his satchel from underneath the table and placed his hand over Cloveris, stroking the leaves.

Ralsky, on noticing Charmzy's distracted expression, leaned over.

"What shall we do?" he asked Charmzy.

Charmzy shifted uncomfortably, his hand still atop the satchel. "I just . . . I can't shake this feeling that something is about to happen."

Crumbzy chimed in while continuing to chew on a large bite of pork. "Why yes, I'm about to lose my head!" Crumbzy gave a nervous laugh, his eyes darting at the emerald-studded axe and King Olaf who was watching them, awaiting the appearance of Cloveris.

"I'm waiting!" the king said.

Charmzy's unease grew stronger. The air in the hall seemed to change, becoming dense and heavy. A soft, almost imperceptible hum filled everyone's ears, resonating from inside the satchel. Charmzy reached into the bag, carefully pulling out the four-leaf clover. His hands glowed with an unearthly green.

King Olaf's eyes sparked with questions as he backed away from the chair where Crumbzy sat, his eyes locked on the clover.

"What? What is that?" the King asked.

As Charmzy held it in his hands, a strange warmth radiated from it, slowly spreading up his arms and into his chest.

"Cloveris . . . what's happening?" Charmzy whispered. But the clover remained silent, its leaves trembling faintly as if responding to something beyond its comprehension.

Suddenly, the warmth intensified. Charmzy's grip tightened as a blinding light began to spread from Cloveris, glowing stronger by the second. The hall fell silent as the feast was forgotten and every eye turned toward the brilliant light radiating not only from the four-leaf clover but from Charmzy's hands and chest.

"Charmzy!" Ralsky shouted. As Charmzy stood up, a light filled the room, causing everyone to shield their eyes. The light pulsed, brighter and brighter, until Charmzy could no longer hold onto the clover. He dropped it onto the table, stumbling back as the light exploded in a burst of radiance.

The shockwave knocked plates and goblets to the floor, sending food scattering in every direction. The king's warriors scrambled to their feet, drawing their weapons in alarm. The waitstaff dropped to the floor and covered their ears, and Jack the Jester ran screaming down the hallway. The king, though, remained standing behind Crumbzy, his eyes mesmerized in amazement.

And then, just as suddenly as it had begun, the light faded.

In its place, a young man stood on top of the banquet table, a figure tall and proud, with broad shoulders, and a well-toned body, shimmering with a soft, ethereal glow. The young man's hair was a vivid shade of green, slicked back and styled with precision. His knickers were made of a silky fabric in a rich, deep wood color, and his shirt, tucked neatly inside, was a pristine white. Hanging from his neck was a pendant shaped like a four-leaf clover, its center adorned with the same diamond that had once been Cloveris' heart.

The young man approached Charmzy and, kneeling on one knee, held the leprechaun's hands in his extended palms.

"Charmzy," he said softly, his voice familiar yet new. "It is I, Cloveris."

The room was still, the air heavy with anticipation.

Charmzy stilled his breath. His hands trembled in Cloveris' palms and his eyes widened in disbelief.

"Cloveris? Is it really you?" His voice shook with awe and uncertainty.

Cloveris' eyes held a shimmering glow as he looked at him. "It's hard to explain, Charmzy. My time as a clover—it wasn't just dormancy. I was waiting. Trapped, yes, but still aware in a way. The clover was my form, but my essence, my spirit . . . it was always more. When you touched the magic within you, it triggered something deep inside me. I felt the pull of being called to bloom into a young man."

Charmzy blinked, still processing what had occurred. "But how? How did you go from clover . . . to this?"

Cloveris smiled softly and said, "I was bound to that clover as a vessel—a guardian of old magic, perhaps even ancient. When you awakened your magic, you unknowingly gave me life. The leaves, the clover—they were a reflection of the magic I held, but my true form was waiting to be unlocked. Your magic was the key."

Charmzy frowned, still uncertain. "So, you're not . . . a clover anymore?"

"Not entirely," Cloveris answered, his voice growing even gentler. "The essence of the clover is still within me. Its magic flows through my body like a memory woven into my soul. But now, I am more—this form . . . this ethereal body is my blooming stage. As you can see, I have become a young man with vitality. I am freed by your great power source."

Cloveris smiled warmly. His eyes sparkled with the same kindness that had always lived within the clover.

The hall remained in stunned silence, the transformation leaving everyone speechless. Crumbzy dropped his fork, his mouth hanging open as he stared at the human form of Cloveris.

Ralsky blinked and rubbed his eyes as if to make sure that what he was seeing was real. "Well, I'll be . . . the little clover's a man now."

King Olaf, who had been watching closely, gazed at Cloveris with an air of solemn respect.

"A transformation like this is not something to be taken lightly," he said, his voice low and commanding. "This magic is powerful . . . ancient."

Cloveris nodded. "It is, Your Majesty. With great honor, I introduce myself as Cloveris, a magical being who has returned from a slumber of fifteen years.

"Are you from the family of Clovers?" King Olaf asked, his voice filled with curiosity.

"Why yes," Cloveris replied, surprised. "I am one of the last of the Clovers. Do you know of my family?"

"Indeed. My father, King Haldor, once found and protected one of your kind," King Olaf recounted. "Her name was Sylvi, which in Norse means 'of the forest.' My father loved her deeply, though they could never be together. The celestial realms would not allow it."

"Ahem, that's an interesting story," Cloveris said.

"For another time, perhaps. Shall we get back to the magic? So, was it you, Cloveris, who stopped my soldiers with a magical shield?" King Olaf questioned.

"Why, Your Majesty, it was not," he responded. "Charmzy may be the key to unlocking this untapped magical potential. I believe he accidentally created that wall."

"So, you don't say?" the king said, sounding intrigued. "How can we discover his hidden magic, Cloveris?"

"With enough introspection and determination, he may be able to create a unique form of magic that he has yet to discover," Cloveris said.

Cloveris turned to Charmzy. "Okay, Charmzy, with deep determination, try to create something to unlock your hidden potential."

Charmzy, still reeling from the shock, responded, "Cloveris . . . I do not know what to say. This is craziness. I have no power. If I had any power, I would have known by now." He continued addressing Cloveris with sorrow in his voice. "You knew of my father. Did he have magical powers? And if he had powers, why did they not prevent him from dying?"

"Charmzy, you must not compare your hidden potential to your father's. It's true, he was conquered even though he had magical gifts. But your gifts are different. You must find the will inside to unlock *your* gifts. Now, concentrate." Cloveris directed with calmness.

Ralsky looked across the table in disbelief and wondered, if this leprechaun really did have magical powers, would he discover that he and Crumbzy were here to steal his gold?

"Leave him alone!" Ralsky said. His commanding voice echoed through the dimly lit room.

"We have had a long and arduous evening, and we have more ahead tomorrow. We must not drain Charmzy. We could all use some much-needed rest. We kindly ask our Majesty to provide us with three horses so we can continue our journey at dawn."

The air was tense as his words hung in the air, waiting for a response.

The king pondered Ralsky's request, his furrowed brow suggesting deep contemplation. After a moment, he said, "Why yes, I am a man of my word. I shall instruct my men to set you up with everything you need for your horses and equip them with the necessary goods for the journey ahead. However, before you depart, I expect all of you to return with the knowledge of any magic that would be useful to my kingdom. Furthermore, I must insist that you return my horses to me upon completion of your journey."

"Certainly, Your Majesty. We are friends, and if I have any magic that could benefit your kingdom in the future, I would be happy to assist my friend in need," Charmzy replied with graciousness.

King Olaf raised his goblet and took a sip of the rich red wine, savoring its flavor before addressing the group again. "Alas, the mystery of the magical wall may forever elude us," he said, his voice heavy with contemplation. Then, with renewed warmth, he lifted his goblet high.

"To friendship!" he declared, his voice ringing through the hall.

The others followed suit, grabbing their glasses and raising them up in solidarity.

"To friendship!" The words echoed in the grand hall as the camaraderie of the moment settled over them.

As the evening drew to a close, the men bid each other goodnight and retreated to the warmth of their beds, the anticipation of the journey ahead filling their hearts. Yet, despite his tiredness and the comfort of the bed, Charmzy found little rest. He tossed and turned, his thoughts heavy with doubts, until at last exhaustion overtook him and he slipped into a dream.

In the depths of his slumber, a soft, ethereal voice called to Charmzy from beyond the veil of sleep.

"Charmzy . . . Charmzy! I'm here. It would be best if you hurried as time is of the essence. We have awaited your presence for too long. The time has come for you to break the curse."

The voice was urgent and filled with a deep sorrow that tugged at his heart. Confused, he squinted into the misty images of his dream while the voice continued.

"The Maldren spirits are rising again. They seek to destroy the mystical realm that safeguards the world's riches and maintains the balance of nature. Your magic—your connection to the rainbow—is the key to stopping them and freeing the ethereal beings."

Charmzy's confusion deepened. "I . . . I do not understand," he said.

A steady but rushed voice replied, "The rainbow is the bridge between the physical world you live in and the Celestial Realm where I reside along with all other magical beings. Your grandfather, Ciaran, was able to harness ancient powers. He became the chosen guardian of this bridge in your world. Now, that responsibility falls to you."

Charmzy felt his pulse quicken. "But what am I supposed to do?" he asked, his voice trembling with uncertainty.

"You must learn to harness the elemental balance," the voice instructed firmly.

"What does that mean?" Charmzy asked as curiosity mingled with his fear.

"Each color of the rainbow corresponds to an element," the voice explained. "Green represents the forests, blue is for the oceans and rivers, yellow for the sun and moon, red for fire, violet for the spirits, while indigo . . . indigo controls darkness and evil."

Charmzy's head spun as the information sank in and the weight of the task pressed down on him.

"The pendulum of power has swung toward evil," the voice continued, dark and foreboding. "The other elements are beginning to wither. If you do not stop the Maldren spirits, all of life will be forever broken and in darkness. The bridge between the physical and Celestial Realms will collapse. And without that bridge, the world will lose its colorful magic forever."

A shiver crawled down Charmzy's spine as the voice whispered the names that sent fear through his veins. "Madison and Winfred grow more powerful with every passing day. Their influence is spreading and driving the world towards destruction."

"How am I supposed to fight them?" Charmzy asked, desperation creeping into his voice.

"The Dark Guardian . . ." the voice said sorrowfully. "The Celestial Realm is sealed off from the rainbow, and I can only communicate with you through your dreams—on nights when the full moon shines. But you, Charmzy, are not powerless. You have the magic of your ancestors and the Clover family within you. Learn to wield it, and stop Madison and Winfred before it is too late."

Charmzy jolted awake. His heart raced as the words of the ethereal being echoed in his mind—Elemental Balance . . . the Maldren spirits . . . Dark Guardian . . . Madison and Winfred. Sweat clung to his skin despite the chill of the early morning air seeping into his chamber. He sat up, clutching his chest.

The room was quiet except for the faint crackle of a fire in the corner as Charmzy contemplated how he could find his magic in time to fight what was to come his way.

CLOVERIS

Chapter Eight
Allies and Revelations

There was a knock at the door. Ralsky entered without waiting for an invitation, his usual reckless self. "Charmzy! Are you awake? We're leaving soon. King Olaf has prepared the horses."

Charmzy nodded, still dazed. He tried to find the right words, but Ralsky was already rummaging through his things and urging him to get up out of bed. "What's got you so pale? Don't tell me the Viking food didn't sit well with you. We have a long journey ahead. No time for your stomach to be playing tricks."

Charmzy hesitated, wondering how much to tell his friends about the dream. Would they believe him or dismiss it as just another bizarre occurrence in a land filled with magic?

"Ralsky," Charmzy began, his voice unsure. "There's something I need to discuss with everyone before we depart. Something . . . important."

Ralsky paused, looking up from his bag. "Go on then, tell me first."

Before Charmzy could speak, Crumbzy barged in with his usual enthusiasm, crumbs of bread already covering his tunic. "Did you hear? King Olaf's cook packed us a whole basket of food for the journey! I was thinking we could—"

Charmzy interrupted, his voice suddenly firm. "I had a dream. A dream about . . . my grandfather. And about the rainbow."

Both gnomes paused, eyes widening. They knew better than to brush it off.

"It wasn't just any dream," Charmzy continued, a trace of urgency creeping into his tone. "It was the voice of Angel Christel. She told me she was trapped on the other side of the rainbow and that the Maldren spirits want to gain the power to destroy and take over all the realms. And . . . I'm supposed to stop them."

Ralsky frowned, then crossed his arms and paced the room. "The Maldren spirits? Never thought I'd hear that name outside of dark tavern tales."

Charmzy nodded grimly. "And worse—Madison and Winfred are growing stronger every day. I don't know how I'm supposed to stop them, but I have to. They want to sever the rainbow bridge between our world and the Celestial Realm."

"Well, that's just perfect, isn't it? We are out here chasing gold, and now we have a cosmic battle on our hands, too," Crumbzy said.

"I don't know if I'm ready," Charmzy admitted, his voice wavering as he looked between his two companions.

Ralsky put a hand on Charmzy's shoulder. "You have always been ready. You just did not know it. And besides, you have us."

At that moment, Cloveris entered the room, his presence instantly commanding the group's attention. His ethereal glow had dimmed but the wisdom in his eyes remained. He walked over to Charmzy, sensing the tension in the air.

"I couldn't help but overhear," Cloveris said, his gaze settling on Charmzy. "You needn't worry. You're not alone in this. You have the potential for great magic, more than you realize. I will mentor you on our journey. Together, we will unlock the power that lies within you."

Charmzy swallowed hard. "But I have never had any real magic before. I thought I could . . . use the rainbow to get gold, to help my mother. I was only a boy back then, chasing dreams. But now . . . this is bigger. It's not just about gold anymore. It is about saving the rainbow. About saving the world."

Ralsky and Crumbzy exchanged glances. They had always chased the dream of treasures, but this was different. They could see that in Charmzy's eyes. It wasn't about riches anymore—it was about something far more important.

"You're right," Ralsky said, nodding slowly. "We need to stop thinking about the gold. This is bigger than us, bigger than any treasure."

Crumbzy rubbed the back of his neck, displaying a rare look of seriousness on his face. "Well, when you put it like that . . . saving the rainbow sounds a bit more . . . heroic. Guess we're in for the long haul, aren't we?"

Cloveris smiled warmly. "You are not the only one with magic, Charmzy. Ralsky and Crumbzy have their gifts as well. Each of you possesses a unique power whether you have tapped into it yet or not."

Crumbzy looked startled. "Wait—are you saying we've got magic too?"

Cloveris nodded. "Gnomes have a deep connection to the earth. Ralsky, your strength and quick thinking are manifestations of that. Crumbzy, your knack for sensing things before they happen is not just luck. It's magic, too."

Ralsky raised an eyebrow. "So, we are . . . magical? Who knew?"

Cloveris continued, "On the journey to Hemlock Circle, we will practice harnessing these powers together as a team. The elements of the rainbow are connected to all living things, and you three are part of that balance. Our combined magic will be key to facing Madison and Winfred."

Charmzy looked at Cloveris, a mixture of fear and hope swirling inside him. "You really think I can do this?"

Cloveris placed a reassuring hand on his shoulder. "I know you can. You must stop with the self-doubt. It weakens your magic. Soon you'll see that your magic and our magical talents will be stronger than anything you could have imagined."

Crumbzy gave a slight, nervous grin. "Well, if we're practicing magic on the way, I hope there's room for error. I don't want to hurt myself."

Ralsky laughed, slapping Crumbzy on the back. "I guess we'll find out soon enough. Let's get to the banquet table. King Olaf awaits us."

As the four made their way to the banquet table, they found King

Olaf deep in thought. The king was pacing around the room with his index finger and thumb neatly placed underneath his chin while tugging at his fiery red beard. Just behind him was Jester Jack, oddly mimicking the king's expression of concern.

"Good morning, King Olaf," Charmzy greeted.

"I trust you had a good night's rest before your departure?" the king replied.

"As best as I could," Charmzy answered, even while his thoughts lingered on the dream still clinging to his mind.

"Well," King Olaf said, gesturing to Jack, "Jack has ensured all the horses are packed and ready for your journey. However, I must warn you that the woods beyond these walls are treacherous and one misstep could prove fatal. If you seek to vanquish the powerful evil force that guards Hemlock Circle, you must not take this task lightly. It will require all your skills. Your magic may be the key to your success."

Cloveris responded, "We understand, Your Majesty. We know the danger. We also know Charmzy is the chosen one—the only one who, with the help of us all, can stop the curse . . . the dark magic plaguing our forests."

King Olaf stopped pacing, his eyes widening. "The chosen one?"

"Why yes," Cloveris said with quiet certainty. "The Celestial Realm anointed his grandfather, Ciaran, to protect and guard what's within the Hemlock Circle—the rainbow. Charmzy is his descendant . . . of Cloverborn lineage."

"The Great Ciaran?" King Olaf stood even taller, his astonishment clear. "Ciaran is his grandfather?" He paused. "Ciaran is a legend. He fought alongside my father, King Haldor. From this day forward, we are allies—just as our families were many ages ago. My father and your grandfather went to battle together against the Malrends."

The four men listened intently as King Olaf continued, "You see, the dark sorcery—black magic, whatever you wish to call it—is used to harm anyone who dares enter the woods in search of the rainbow. Spells have been cast on the birds, directing them to watch for anyone looking for Hemlock Circle, and they report their findings to the dark realm. Even the trees seem enchanted, their gnarled branches leaning in to eavesdrop on conversations. Just mentioning gold, the rainbow, or Hemlock Circle creates a signal that travels through the woods, alerting every creature and dark spirit."

Ralsky, growing increasingly skeptical, snorted, "This is hogwash! Trees and birds talking?"

King Olaf's eye twitched as his voice turned sharp. "Listen to me, you pipsqueak gnome. Your kind has always been selfish, consumed by greed. For centuries, the gnomes have been cursed—forever chasing after the gold of Hemlock."

Ralsky's face flushed a deep red. His anger brimmed just beneath the surface from the king's insults. Charmzy quickly stepped in.

"I understand the gnomes' desire for gold, King Olaf, but these two gnomes—Ralsky and Crumbzy—are in this for more than just treasure. They're part of something bigger now."

The king's eyes bore into Charmzy and his expression softened slightly. "Mark my words, Charmzy. When you gain access to the rainbow, be cautious. Magic like this can turn anyone dark quickly, even with the best intentions."

Charmzy was taken aback by the thought of his friends possibly succumbing to the allure of dark magic. A sense of unease crept over him, but he soon composed himself.

"My friends," he said cautiously, "perhaps we should heed the king's warning. We must take care not to speak of our destination aloud. If the birds and trees can honestly communicate our whereabouts to Winfred and Madison, we'd be putting ourselves in danger."

Crumbzy scratched his head with a sheepish grin. "Well, that might be a bit hard for me. You know I tend to blurt things out."

The king, whose expression had turned serious, stepped toward Crumbzy and glanced back at the group. "Men, I want to offer you every possible aid in your battle against the black magic. To that end, I shall furnish you with a helper."

Jack the Jester, who had been lingering in the corner with a mischievous grin, suddenly perked up. He eagerly stepped forward, a gleeful twinkle in his eye. "Your Majesty," Jack said with a theatrical bow, "I'd be honored to—"

"Jack," the king interrupted with a firm yet kind smile, "not you. Please, bring Thunderbolt to us at once."

Both gnomes, who had tensed up at the thought of traveling with the jester, released a sigh of relief, their puffed chests relaxing. They exchanged a glance, thankful that Jack would not be their guide on this perilous journey.

Momentarily deflated, Jack quickly recovered his composure. He cleared his throat and said, "Ahem, yes, Your Majesty." Then, he dashed up the grand staircase, his footsteps echoing through the hall. Moments later, he returned carrying a large and ornately gilded birdcage.

Inside stood a magnificent golden eagle, its regal presence immediately commanding the attention of everyone in the room. The bird's body was massive, its sharp talons gleaming like polished steel. As it spread its wings, which spanned an incredible nine feet, the golden feathers shimmered in the light like molten gold, making the creature appear almost ghostly. Its bright amber and copper eyes radiated intelligence and power. Around its neck, it wore a finely-crafted golden collar engraved with a Viking insignia, its name, "Thunderbolt," etched above.

"Allow me to introduce Thunderbolt," King Olaf said with pride. "He is my most loyal companion and a pet that I trust with my life. Thunderbolt will guide you safely to Hemlock Circle. His sharp eyes will spot any danger before it reaches you. Should you need my assistance, Thunderbolt can swiftly return to me with a message. You can trust him completely. He will be your faithful and reliable companion throughout your journey."

Crumbzy's usual boldness was replaced with awe as the gnome slowly approached the cage and offered a greeting. "Hello there, Thunderbolt. It's . . . um . . . an honor to meet you."

Thunderbolt gazed at Crumbzy for a moment before letting out a loud piercing squawk that echoed through the hall. The sound sent a shiver down Crumbzy's spine, but he smiled awkwardly, backing up a step.

King Olaf chuckled as he opened the golden cage. Thunderbolt leaped from inside, then he spread his wings and soared gracefully around the room before flying out through the palace doors into the open sky. The gnomes and Charmzy watched in awe as the golden eagle circled the palace, his flight both powerful and graceful, a promise of protection and guidance. "Follow him," King Olaf instructed. "Thunderbolt will ensure that your path remains true."

Chapter Nine
The Cursed Forest

As the hours passed, the four men continued their journey on horseback through the cursed forest. What was once a thriving landscape filled with vibrant trees had been reduced to a desolate wasteland. The creatures that once thrived now struggled to survive, and most animals and the bees had vanished with the sunlight and water. Hemlock Forest, now known as The Woods of Hemlock, was no longer a place of life. The black magic had left the forest barren, where nothing grew, and hope had withered alongside the trees.

The travelers followed the golden eagle as it glided between the trees. Occasionally, Ralsky would glance upward to watch Thunderbolt catch prey with swift precision. "Hey boys, seeing Thunderbolt grab that mouse has reminded me—it's about lunchtime for us," Ralsky called out, breaking the silence.

Crumbzy's stomach growled loudly in agreement. "Yes, I'm so hungry I'd eat that mouse too," he joked, rubbing his belly.

Charmzy nodded. "Let's stop for a break by that large log ahead."

The group dismounted and gathered around the log. Thunderbolt perched on a branch above them, ever watchful. As they pulled food from their satchels and settled onto the log, Crumbzy turned to Cloveris.

"Have you ever touched the gold? Seen the Hemlock Rainbow?" he asked, his mouth full of bread.

"No, I haven't," Cloveris replied.

Before Crumbzy could ask another question, the log beneath them shifted slightly.

"Did you feel that?" asked Charmzy, looking around.

"Feel what?" replied Ralsky, glancing up from his meal.

The tree above them bent inward, its dried branches creaking as they leaned toward the group, almost as if eavesdropping. Ralsky frowned and muttered, "Crumbzy, did you forget to shut your mouth?"

"What? I'm just asking about the gold!" Crumbzy replied, clearly irritated.

Cloveris placed his long fingers over Crumbzy's mouth. Then Crumbzy's eyes widened in realization, his thoughts catching up to King Olaf's warning. The trees were alive, listening—and now, leaning closer.

Suddenly, Thunderbolt swooped down from his perch, squawking and flapping his wings in a fury as if trying to silence Crumbzy himself. The tree's branches whipped forward, trying to swat Thunderbolt away, but the eagle was too fast and shot back into the sky. The log the men were sitting on began to bounce as the ground beneath them shook.

A woman's voice, unfamiliar and strong, rang out, "Get your lumps off my trunk!" Startled, the men yelped and leaped from the log. Ralsky, his eyes wide, muttered, "Well, King Olaf wasn't kidding. These trees are alive—and they're listening."

Crumbzy groaned. "I'm such a nincompoop. My big mouth has gotten us in trouble again."

Cloveris stood tall, spreading his arms in a gesture of peace. "We mean you no harm," he said to the trees. "Let me introduce myself. I am Cloveris, once a four-leaf clover, now human. And these are my companions, Charmzy, Ralsky, and Crumbzy."

A soft voice replied, "Hello. I'm Anne, the chestnut tree you were sitting on. I'm sorry for startling you, but I've suffered greatly from the curse on this forest. The dark magic has left me weak and I'm slowly dying."

Charmzy approached the tree, placing his hand on its trunk. "I'm so sorry, Anne. What happened to you?"

Before she could reply, a more profound and deep voice interrupted, "Stop at once! You'll get us all punished!"

A nearby tree tilted forward, its branches brushing against Charmzy's shoulder. "The curse brought by Winfred and Madison has already done its damage. But we must report anyone talking of gold," the tree added sternly.

"Who are you?" Cloveris asked, his eyes narrowing.

"I'm Sherman," the deep voice rumbled. "And this is my brother, Cyrus." A lower branch extended its reach towards Charmzy as if offering a handshake.

"Well, hello there, little leprechaun," Cyrus said. "Are you here to rescue our forest?"

"Oh my! Could it be?" Anne gasped, her branches swaying. "Will you save us?"

Sherman remained suspicious. "We cannot trust them. Just mentioning gold can bring punishment from Winfred and Madison. We must report this at once!"

Ralsky stepped forward, scowling. "No one's reporting anything, or I'll turn you into firewood to keep us warm at night!"

The trees trembled at his threat.

"Peace, Ralsky," Cloveris interjected. "We are here to help, not harm. Charmzy is no ordinary leprechaun. He has magic—he's the one who transformed me from clover to human."

The trees gasped in surprise.

"If you do not report them, we will all face punishment," Sherman insisted, though doubt lingered in his voice. "Just look at Anne, barely clinging to life."

Cypress sighed. "We need courage. If Charmzy truly is the chosen one, we must stand with him. Otherwise, we are doomed to live in this wasteland forever."

Cloveris turned to Charmzy and placed a hand on his shoulder. "The time has come, Charmzy. You must summon your magic—pull from your heart and mind. Together, we can heal this forest."

Charmzy closed his eyes, and Cloveris did the same. A brilliant aura of light surrounded them, spreading out in waves. Slowly, the light enveloped Anne. Her trunk straightened, her branches lifted, and her roots dug deeply into the earth, reestablishing their connection with the soil. Within moments, she was restored, her chestnut leaves flourishing once more.

"I can't believe it," she whispered. "You are the chosen one . . . here to save us." Anne breathed a sigh of relief as she lifted her blossoming branches.

Cyrus added, "Yes, he is the chosen one. We must help him reach his destination."

Sherman frowned. "But dark magic always finds a way to alert the Witch and Warlock. They are aware of everything that happens in the Woods of Hemlock."

Cyprus nodded. "True, Sherman. But with the help of the trees, we can offer them some protection. We must hurry before Winfred and Madison discover their presence."

Cloveris stepped forward, addressing the group. "This is only the beginning. Charmzy, Ralsky, Crumbzy—you all have magic within you. The journey ahead will require more than just strength. It will take all our combined powers. With the help of the trees, we can defeat Winfred and Madison. We must practice harnessing our gifts."

Ralsky raised an eyebrow. "We've got magic too?"

"Yes," Cloveris explained. "You, Ralsky, have a deep connection with the earth. You can sense its vibrations, and you can use this to detect dangers ahead. And my senses tell me you also have a talent for the magic of illusion. Crumbzy, your enhanced senses allow you to feel shifts in the air, and you are excellent in alchemy and engineering. You have quick reflexes that aren't just luck. They are magical, too."

Crumbzy blinked in surprise. "I've got magic, like engineering and alchemy?"

Cloveris nodded. "Yes. And together we'll practice on our journey to Hemlock Circle. It's time to harness the full potential of our combined abilities."

Meanwhile, back at Black Rock Castle, Warlock Winfred hovered over his crystal ball on Majestic Mountain. His dark robe swirled around him as he exclaimed, "Look at who's back! What do we have here?" As he gazed into the crystal ball, it glowed with an eerie light, revealing a group of four in the Woods of Hemlock: a leprechaun, a young man, and two gnomes. The crystal ball gave him only a glimpse of the scene. He could not make out the figures and their surroundings nor hear what was being said through his crystal.

Winfred knew that the travelers were up to something and was determined to find out what it was. "My dear Chelsea, fetch Madison. We need her insights this time."

Madison, a petite and enigmatic figure, entered the room as soon as Chelsea called out to her. Her hair was as black as the night sky. Straight and shiny, it cascaded down in long silky strands that framed her face perfectly. Her high cheekbones, full lips, and dainty nose added to her unique beauty. But what truly set her apart were her eyes. They were as blue as the most transparent summer sky and had a pale, ghostly quality. "What is it, my brother?" she asked.

Winfred pointed at the crystal ball and explained, "We have visitors, Madison. Two gnomes, a peculiar green-haired boy, and a leprechaun. The question is—who are they?"

Madison's gaze turned inward as she concentrated, reaching out to her mystical powers. "Let me call upon Thomas, the luminary," she said with a determined look.

From her desk, Madison retrieved a witch board with a luminous face. She tapped it three times and said, "Thomas, awaken."

A face of light appeared on the board and responded in a deep voice, "How may I assist you, beautiful Madison?"

"Thank you, Thomas. Tell me, who are these four men in The Woods of Hemlock? Could one of them be the chosen one?" she inquired, her voice composed and serene.

"The chosen one is among them, but only one," replied the luminous face, resonating with wisdom.

Madison's interest was piqued, and she asked, "Tell me, noble Thomas, who is the chosen one among them?"

The voice responded clearly, "Charmzy Cloverborn."

Winfred's expression shifted from curiosity to disbelief. "Did he just say what I think he said? Cloverborn?"

Madison nodded and, in a voice tinged with awe, said, "Yes, my brother. Charmzy Cloverborn."

Winfred's memory resurfaced. "I thought we brought an end to the Cloverborns—Finn and Ciaran, those two pesky leprechauns. I took care of them."

Madison cleared her throat. "We . . . my brother. We took care of them." Then, a sly smile spread across her face. "Ah, yes—Finn Cloverborn. How could we ever forget him?" She laughed out loud.

Winfred simmered with anger. "Yes, he tried to destroy us and steal our powers from within the Hemlock Rainbow—but not for long." He let out a wicked laugh. "The gold that rightfully belongs to me is hidden beyond the Hemlock Rainbow, along with even greater power. And now, it seems, we must deal with this Charmzy Cloverborn. We can't let him break the dark magic we've secured."

Winfred called out for Chelsea and the crimson red-tail hawk swooped in on his shoulder. "Yes, Master?"

"You must go at once to the Woods of Hemlock and listen to what transpires with this leprechaun named Charmzy Cloverborn. Then, report to me immediately if there is something of great importance regarding my rainbow," Warlock Winfred instructed.

"Yes, Master." Then Chelsea flew from the window towards the Woods of Hemlock in search of a leprechaun.

Back in the Woods of Hemlock, Thunderbolt was on watch high above the tops of the trees. Suddenly, his sharp ears picked up the sound of a nearby squawk. His keen eyesight scanned the area, and he soon spotted his archenemy, Chelsea, perched on a tree overlooking Charmzy and his mates. She was a magnificent red-tailed eagle, her feathers a deep shade of crimson that glinted in the dim skylight and her eyes a deep golden yellow. Her piercing eyes focused intently on the group below, and Thunderbolt knew she was up to no good.

Thunderbolt and Chelsea had once been inseparable, soaring together through the lush Hemlock Forest—now a desolate wasteland. Raised under the care of Winfred and Madison, who had once been loving, the two were treated as prized companions. But as the witch and warlock grew obsessed with power, they became consumed by their ego and vanity.

Their magic, once used to nurture the forest, became a tool of destruction. If the creatures of Hemlock failed to protect the rainbow and its gold, Winfred and Madison unleashed their wrath. Fires tore through the woods, and hurricanes and tornadoes ravaged the land for days. Many animals were forced to flee while others perished in the chaos.

One fateful evening a band of Irish leprechauns arrived searching for the Hemlock Rainbow. Thunderbolt watched in shock as Winfred transformed into a monstrous dragon. Descending from the mountains in a fit of rage, Winfred unleashed his fury, raining fire upon the forest and its inhabitants. Thunderbolt looked on in horror as flames devoured trees and leprechauns alike while Madison struck down creatures with a flick of her wrist or summoned cyclones to sweep them away without mercy.

Caught in the conflict, Thunderbolt tried to protect his friends. He was injured, his wing torn in the crossfire. King Olaf saved him, recognizing the eagle's strength and spirit. Under the Viking king's care, Thunderbolt healed and was trained to become a Viking hawk tasked with protecting the kingdom. Though he embraced his new role, Thunderbolt never forgot the pain of his past—or Chelsea, who had remained loyal to Winfred.

Each time Thunderbolt soared through the skies, he longed for Hemlock Forest to return to its former glory. But the once-vibrant woods had become a wasteland, and Chelsea, who had chosen the side of darkness, now served as Winfred's spy.

As Thunderbolt approached Chelsea's perch, his heart heavy with their shared history, he circled her, showing off his aerial prowess in a silent plea for her to remember what they once had. But Chelsea, unimpressed, kept her gaze fixed on the men below, listening to their conversation.

Without warning, Thunderbolt dove toward her, hoping to scare her away, but his aim was off. He collided with her, sending Chelsea tumbling from the branch. Horror gripped Thunderbolt as he watched her limp form fall through the air. Acting on instinct, he swooped down and caught her just before she hit the ground.

Thunderbolt searched frantically for a safe place to lay her down.

Finally, he found a small, secluded area and gently placed her body there, unconscious and vulnerable. As he hovered nearby, guilt weighed heavily on him. He hoped she would recover soon, hoped there was still a chance to save her, just as King Olaf had once saved him.

In the meantime, the trees Charmzy had befriended huddled together, their branches rustling as they whispered among themselves. They discussed how they could aid Charmzy and communicate with the other creatures in the forest now that the chosen one had arrived. He listened closely as Sherman, one of the oldest trees in the forest, spoke up.

"Listen carefully to me, Charmzy," he said, his voice deep and resonant. "Winfred and Madison have frightening powers, but they're under the influence of some dark magic. Madison was once a pure-hearted white witch and the warlock Winfred walked through our forest with joy. However, discovering the hidden Hemlock Rainbow changed them forever. They returned from their journey altered. We have all sensed the darkness surrounding them."

Cyrus chimed in. "Yes, it lies within the Hemlock Rainbow, where the spell can be broken. You must find your way into the rainbow before they stop you."

Anne expressed her heartfelt gratitude. "Thank you, Charmzy, for bringing me back to life. I feel a renewed strength in my roots because of your divine magic. The trees will send out a message to all living beings in the forest to join forces with you and defeat the wickedness that has brought about the destruction of Hemlock Forest."

Sherman was filled with urgency as he shouted, "Go now!"

The four men mounted their horses and Charmzy tightened his grip on the reins. "We'll save this forest. I swear it."

With Thunderbolt soaring ahead, the group galloped deeper into the forest, heading straight for Hemlock Circle.

Meanwhile, Chelsea, the red-tailed eagle, began to stir, dizzy and disoriented. She soon remembered how Thunderbolt had knocked her off her perch while she was eavesdropping on the men's conversation. Seething with anger, Chelsea prepared to demand answers from the trees about what had transpired with the leprechaun—or make them suffer the consequences.

When the trees saw Chelsea approaching, they immediately agreed they could help Charmzy by delaying the eagle.

"Well, hello there, Chelsea! You are looking absolutely beautiful today," said Anne. "Your wings are breathtaking. How do you keep them looking so shiny and lovely?"

Chelsea dusted away the debris from her fall and smiled. "Thank you for noticing. My Master Winfred takes excellent care of me. He ensures I bathe regularly and conditions my wings weekly to keep them looking their best."

The trees nodded in agreement and praised Master Winfred for his excellent care of Chelsea.

"I saw a skinny leprechaun and some other characters chatting here a while ago," said Chelsea.

Cyrus responded, "I was asleep, but maybe Sherman saw them. Sherman, did you happen to see a leprechaun?

Sherman replied, "It's been so long since I've seen one. I might've forgotten what they look like. Could you give me a description?"

Chelsea scoffed. "Oh, come on, Sherman. You know the type— little Irish fairies, wearing knickers and buckled shoes, always shouting, 'Where's my gold?' Ridiculous top hats and all."

Sherman frowned, feigning confusion. "Hmm, doesn't ring a bell. No, I can't say I've seen any leprechauns around."

As their conversation continued, Chelsea's eyes suddenly widened. "Wait a minute—Anne! You're standing upright! How—?" She circled the chestnut tree in astonishment. "I distinctly remember Madison striking you down. But now, look at you! Your branches are full, and you're rooted firmly in the ground. How did this happen?"

Cyrus replied calmly, "Chelsea, it doesn't matter how. What's important is that Anne has been restored. This is a miracle, considering how long she was severed from the soil, thanks to Madison and Winfred. When will you stop defending their black magic? They've become monsters."

Sherman added in a sharp tone, "Yes, monsters. Thunderbolt witnessed their cruelty firsthand when he helped save the forest creatures during that treacherous fire. Where were you, Chelsea?"

Chelsea lowered her gaze to the ground, shame creeping over her.

Without a word, she spread her wings and bolted into the sky, disappearing into the clouds as she made her way back to Black Rock Castle.

Chapter Ten
Turning Tides

As Chelsea flew through the castle's open window, she expertly navigated the familiar hallways, her wings brushing against the cold stone walls as she sped toward the sitting room. Her heart pounded with urgency, knowing that the news she was carrying would disrupt the delicate balance that had been tenuously maintained. The castle, usually a place of comfort, felt ominous tonight as if it were aware of the approaching storm.

Bursting into the sitting room, Chelsea was met by the warmth of a crackling fire that cast a golden glow over the plush velvet seats. The room was alive with the sounds of laughter and the playful banter of Winfred and Madison who were deeply immersed in their game of cat and mouse. The contrast between their lighthearted play and the heavy burden Chelsea bore was striking.

Winfred, the elder of the two, with his commanding presence and deep, eerie voice, played the villain with practiced ease. His tone dripped with arrogance as he declared, "How dare you touch my gold and how dare you try to take The Hemlock Woods from under my feet!"

With her innocent, wide-eyed expression, Madison matched his intensity with surprising fierceness. In a small but sharp voice, she taunted him. "Why are you standing back? Afraid I'll hurt you . . . with my words? You're an evil warlock! Why do you have to keep turning our forest into a mess every chance you get?"

"Kneel to me, you peasant, or I will chase you out of my woods," Winfred commanded, raising his magic staff. The room seemed to darken as his power surged, filling the air with palpable tension.

Madison, undeterred, stood her ground. "Chase? Did you say chase? I will not leave until I get my gold. If you dare test me, you will regret it."

Winfred's laugh echoed through the room as he transformed into a menacing wolf, his form twisting and enlarging until he towered over Madison. With a growl, he lunged at her, but Madison, quick and resourceful, muttered a spell that transformed her into a tiny mouse. The wolf chased the mouse around the room, their laughter mixing with the fire's crackling as the game continued.

But as the wolf caught the mouse in his paw, about to snap his jaws shut, Madison transformed back into herself. She stood glaring defiantly at Winfred. "How dare you," she exclaimed, her eyes shining with a mix of anger and amusement. "You would eat your own sister!"

Winfred reverted to his human form, laughing heartily. "Only in jest, dear Madison. I would never harm you."

It was then that Winfred noticed Chelsea perched by the window, her feathers ruffled, her eyes wide with the urgency of her message. "Oh, look who has finally arrived. Why, hello, Chelsea. Where have you been all evening?" Winfred's voice was casual, but his eyes narrowed slightly, sensing something was amiss. "What news do you bring from the Woods of Hemlock? Surely, you've heard whispers of the leprechaun?"

Chelsea hesitated as her sharp eyes met Winfred's. She could feel the weight of his gaze as if he were trying to peer into her soul. She knew she had to be careful with her words.

"Master Winfred, I did not find the leprechaun and the trees . . . the trees would not speak to me."

Madison narrowed her eyes, her suspicion evident. "You're lying," she accused. Her voice, usually playful, had taken on a dangerous edge.

But Winfred placed a calming hand on his sister's shoulder and said, "Chelsea would never lie. She is a loyal member of our family."

Madison wasn't convinced. With a flick of her wrist, she summoned her witch board, Thomas. The board floated into her hands, its surface glowing with an eerie light as she tapped it to life. "Thomas," she called out, her voice dripping with sweetness and malice.

The board's luminous eyes blinked, and a smooth, velvety voice emerged. "Yes, my beautiful Madison. What may I do for you this evening?"

Madison's gaze remained fixed on Chelsea. "Dear Thomas, are we in the presence of a liar?"

The eyes on the board scanned the room before locking onto Chelsea.

"You are harboring a traitor," Thomas declared, his voice reverberating through the room. "The pet is not honest."

Winfred's expression darkened, his eyes blazing with anger as they fixed on Chelsea. Madison's lips curled into a smirk.

"See, Winfred? Now, Chelsea, tell us where the leprechaun is, or I will turn you into a mouse," Madison threatened.

Chelsea ruffled her feathers as her mind raced. "I only . . . I only want to stop you both from ruining any more lives. I saw Thunderbolt and I know he misses the old times we had before . . . before you both changed."

Her voice was thick with emotion. "Please, I beg you, return to your good nature. We were a family. Thunderbolt and I were your beloved ones until you sent him away with your dragon's breath."

Madison's face twisted in anger. "How dare you betray your only family, the very hand that feeds and protects you!" With a swift motion, she sent the board flying back to the desk and began chanting a spell, her voice low and dangerous.

Winfred, acting quickly, crossed his hands and sealed Madison's lips with a spell.

"Listen carefully, Chelsea," he said, his voice cold and authoritative. "We are protecting our livelihood, our riches, and the power bestowed upon us by the Hemlock Rainbow. It is ours, and it always will be. Anyone who dares to come between us and our wealth will face dire consequences."

He released Madison from the spell who immediately began

hurling insults at Chelsea. "You little good-for-nothing creature! You're not worthy of our family. I could easily crush you."

But Chelsea, perched on her stand, was no longer the fearful bird that had flown into the room. She had made her decision. Then, she began to explain: "I could not receive any information from the forest. The leprechaun and his friends were gone when I arrived. I did see them briefly, but then . . . I was knocked unconscious."

"Unconscious?" Winfred echoed, his brows furrowing.

"Yes, Master. I believe it was Thunderbolt who knocked me down from the tree."

Winfred's expression darkened further and his hand stroked his chin. "That little menacing eagle!" he threatened. "I should have finished him off when I had the chance. But no matter, his time will come."

Chelsea's heart ached. "No! Not Thunderbolt. He is family," she pleaded, her voice breaking.

Winfred looked at Chelsea with iciness in his gaze. "He was never our family. His loyalty was always to the forest, to those who dared to defy us. Thunderbolt chose them over us. For that, he is a traitor."

Madison's voice was as sharp as a blade. "Chelsea, it's time to find this leprechaun—the son of Finn Cloverborn—before he reaches the Hemlock Rainbow. We must go now! Time is of the essence."

Winfred nodded in agreement. "Yes, my sister is right. If he reaches the rainbow tonight, he could shatter our dark powers, and then we'll lose our chance to summon the Malrend family from the dark spirit world."

Without another word, the three of them set out into the night. The castle doors creaked open and the cold night air greeted them as they flew out, the moonlight casting eerie shadows on the ancient stone walls. Winfred and Madison rode on her broom while Chelsea flew just behind them. Chelsea felt conflicted but took to the skies, her keen eyes scanning the forest below for any sign of movement.

The Hemlock Woods, usually alive with the sounds of nocturnal creatures, seemed unnaturally quiet, as if the forest itself was holding its breath. The tall, twisted trees loomed over them, the only sound the gentle swaying of their branches in the breeze. The trees offered no guidance, no warning, and would not whisper their secrets even to Chelsea.

As they pressed deeper into the woods, Madison grew impatient. "Move faster, Winfred," she snapped, gripping her broom tighter. "We don't have time for your hesitation. If we miss him now, we might lose him for good to the rainbow."

Winfred frowned but held on, his voice a low grumble. "I'm not hesitating. I don't want to fall off your blasted broom again."

"Then try holding on for once," Madison shot back, rolling her eyes. "Focus! He's got to be out here somewhere."

Chelsea circled above, still conflicted. Her golden eyes scanned the forest below, piercing through the shadows.

"They can't have gotten far. Where are you hiding, little leprechaun?" Madison hissed, her blue eyes flashing in the darkness. "We must be close. I sense the smell of a leprechaun."

Winfred nodded, his staff glowing faintly. "Stay alert. They're cunning, especially the leprechaun. He's the son of Finn Cloverborn, after all. We need to be ready for anything."

Chelsea finally caught sight of something unusual in a small clearing ahead. She swooped down without a sound and perched on a low branch, watching the scene unfold below.

The men they sought had made camp with the trolls in the heart of the forest. Charmzy sat by the fire, his eyes reflecting the flames as he conversed quietly with his companions. Thunderbolt, majestic and alert, perched beside Charmzy, his eyes scanning the darkness, ever vigilant.

Ralsky muttered under his breath as he poked at the fire with a stick, clearly annoyed by something Crumbzy had done. As he tried to sit down, Crumbzy tripped over a log and nearly toppled into the fire, only to be saved by the swift hand of Cloveris.

Cloveris exuded an air of calm authority. His long, graceful fingers glowed faintly as he conjured small spells to ward off the night's chill. He turned to Charmzy, who sat quietly beside him, his expression a mix of worry and determination.

"You're closer than you think, Charmzy," Cloveris said, his voice soft yet powerful. "The Hemlock Rainbow is near, and with it, your true powers will ignite. I know this to be true. But it would be best if you trusted in yourself. Together, we can overcome whatever Winfred and Madison throw at you."

Charmzy nodded, his heart pounding in his chest. He knew the journey was far from over and the danger was more significant than ever.

Just as Cloveris finished speaking, Thunderbolt let out a low cry of warning. The group tensed as their eyes scanned the darkness beyond the firelight. They knew they weren't alone.

In the shadows, Winfred and Madison watched, biding their time. "Now," Winfred whispered, his voice barely audible. With a flick of his wrist, the staff's glow intensified, casting eerie dancing lights across the trees.

Chelsea felt heaviness in her heart as she watched Winfred and Madison prepare to strike. She knew she had to make a choice. Would she warn the group below, betraying her family? Or would she stay silent and let them attack Thunderbolt and his group?

Just then, Brutus, the giant troll, along with Gramal and the entire troll family sprang up from their cots. They grabbed their handmade weapons and stood shoulder to shoulder to form a protective circle around Charmzy, Ralsky, Crumbzy, and Cloveris. As the tension in the clearing grew, Thunderbolt narrowed his eyes and rustled his wings as he prepared to defend his friends.

Cloveris raised his hands high and cast a bright star into the sky. It streaked across the heavens, illuminating the forest in a dazzling display. The brilliant light revealed the Warlock and the Witch, who stood in stunned silence, their presence now fully exposed. For a fleeting moment, they stood before the leprechaun's band of friends with expressions twisted in anger. Ready to strike, but caught by surprise, they chose to flee.

Madison snapped her fingers, summoning her broom. "Swiftly!" she called out. The broom appeared with a whoosh, and she grabbed her brother by the edge of his cloak, pulling him onto the broom. They shot into the starlit night sky with their devoted red-tailed hawk, Chelsea, following closely behind.

Chelsea felt a wave of relief wash over her as they soared through the night. She was thankful she hadn't been forced to choose between warning Thunderbolt and staying loyal to her family. But deep down, she knew this retreat wouldn't last. The time for confrontation was fast approaching, and the fate of Hemlock Woods hung in the balance.

The tension thickened as the Witch and Warlock returned to Black Rock Castle. Their footsteps echoed ominously through the dark corridors as they made their way to the war room, ready to plan their next move. "They must not reach the tree of Angel Christel—that's where his power lies," Winfred growled. "I tried to burn it down once, but it wouldn't catch fire. If this leprechaun is the chosen one, we could lose everything. The rainbow's shifting towards the dark side. I saw it after the last rain—the indigo is spreading, overtaking the other colors."

Madison's eyes gleamed with a sinister edge. "He cannot be allowed to unlock the rainbow," she said, her voice sharp with urgency. "We must disguise ourselves within Hemlock Circle and watch. If Charmzy Cloverborn is the chosen one, we'll strike before he enters the rainbow."

Chelsea, perched silently beside them, listened intently. Her loyalty to Winfred and Madison had never wavered, but now a flicker of doubt crept into her mind. She knew the depths of their cruelty and feared the destruction that would follow.

"Wait a minute," she interjected. Her voice was cautious and edged with unease. "Do we not want him to unlock the rainbow?"

Winfred arched his brow and rested his palm thoughtfully on his chin. "Good question, Chelsea," he mused. "We haven't crossed over the rainbow since our magic locked us out. But if Angel Christel unlocks it for the chosen one, we could enter and claim the greater treasures within the core."

His eyes gleamed with a sudden realization. Winfred clapped and let out an evil laugh.

"Ha! Ha! You're right, Chelsea. We let the little leprechaun do all the work, then destroy him and his friends once the rainbow is revealed. The riches and powers inside will be ours. And if we turn the rainbow fully indigo, we can call the Malrend spirits back to Earth. Brilliant!"

Madison curled her lips into a wicked smile. "Yes, my brother, you are a genius," she purred, her mind already envisioning the power of the Malrend spirits that awaited them.

However, Chelsea felt a growing dread for asking the question. The idea of more power normally would have thrilled Chelsea, but the thought of what Winfred and Madison might do once they had it filled her with fear. She knew Thunderbolt, now aligned with Charmzy and his companions, would be in grave danger. She needed to warn him, but how could she do so without arousing suspicion?

"We'll retreat to our chambers for now," Winfred commanded with a tone of finality. "We begin tomorrow evening. The fools still have a long road ahead and won't arrive until nightfall. Let's rest and be ready to end this once and for all."

As they parted ways, Chelsea hesitated before following. Her mind raced with conflicting thoughts, torn between her loyalty to Winfred and her fear of what was to come. She knew the time for a decision was drawing near.

"Come along, Chelsea, to my chamber, my trusted little pet." When Winfred extended his elbow towards her to have her jump on, she did as she was told. They retreated to his chamber where he carefully brushed her feathers before bedtime and spoke to her in a confidential tone.

"Chelsea, I'm very excited for what's to come. Who knows what other mystical gifts await me to capture from Hemlock's Rainbow? Do you remember our last time with Angel Christel and those leprechauns?"

"Why yes, Master Winfred, I do recall," Chelsea said.

"And wasn't I magnificent? Of course, Madison was a radiant glow with her new magic, but I can rule the world if I possess more power. I can change everything to agree with me and hold riches beyond the Woods of Hemlock. Which reminds me, I must get word to the trees and all living beings in the forest that if they disobey my commands, I will wage a war of destruction on them for eternity."

Chelsea chimed in, "Master Winfred, I can fly through the night and deliver your message to all who dwell in the forest. The trees and the animals will side with you. We can summon them for the battle."

Winfred gleamed with excitement as he clapped in agreement. "Yes! Yes, Chelsea, fly tonight. Tell them the time has come to choose sides. I choose Indigo!" His voice twisted with madness and a hysterical laugh escaped his lips, echoing through the dark halls of Black Rock Castle.

Without another word, Chelsea spread her wings and launched herself into the cold night sky. But as the wind rushed past her feathers, her heart raced not with loyalty—but with a hidden plan. She wasn't heading to rally the forest creatures for Winfred. She had a different mission.

Chelsea soared high above the treetops toward Nordheimer Castle where King Olaf and his army resided. She knew she had to warn him of the coming danger. Thunderbolt and the leprechaun needed more than just luck and magic—they needed an army.

Meanwhile, back at the trolls' camp, Charmzy and his companions gathered around the dwindling fire. The air was thick with anticipation, and each knew they were nearing the final confrontation.

"We're so close," Ralsky muttered, pacing near the fire, "closer than I'd like. Winfred and Madison won't stop until they've drained the rainbow dry."

Gramal, seated across from them, nodded grimly. "The Warlock and Witch are cunning, and their magic grows stronger by the day. Be warned that the way is filled with illusions and traps meant to confuse those seeking the rainbow. But we trolls know these lands better than anyone. We'll fight alongside you when the time comes."

Charmzy looked around at his friends—the brave trolls, Cloveris, Ralsky, Crumbzy, and Thunderbolt, perched on a branch above them, ever watchful.

"Winfred and Madison are coming for the rainbow," Charmzy said, his voice low but determined. "But we won't let them win."

Chapter Eleven
A Troll's Toll

The group pressed on through the night, winding their way through the cursed Woods of Hemlock. Exhaustion tugged at them, but they focused on reaching the mystical tree shaped like an angel.

As the sun dipped below the horizon, Crumbzy broke the silence. "Look up!" he shouted, pointing towards the sky.

Cloveris, Ralsky, and Charmzy sat astride their horses watching as Thunderbolt swooped and spiraled through the air, his wings beating powerfully. He directed them northward, guiding them toward Hemlock Circle.

"Seems like he's showing us the way," Ralsky said, his excitement growing. "Come on, we're close! To the gold!"

The horses surged forward, racing through the thick brush until a long, narrow wooden bridge came into view. Charmzy, riding ahead, suddenly halted the group with an outstretched arm.

"Hold on, Ralsky!" Charmzy warned, his voice tense. Just as the group stopped, a massive thud reverberated through the air and the fragile bridge trembled. Crumbzy's eyes widened, Cloveris' face filled with curiosity, and Ralsky clenched his jaw, sensing danger. Slowly, Charmzy turned back towards the bridge where a towering and menacing troll stood blocking their path.

"If you want to cross, you must pay the toll," the troll growled, his voice low and threatening.

"We're not paying any toll," Ralsky snapped. But Cloveris stepped forward, ever the diplomat.

"Perhaps you'll kindly allow us to pass and we'll pay you upon our return?" Cloveris suggested, his tone respectful but calm.

The troll's lip coiled into a snarl. "No toll, no passage. Cross without paying, and I'll eat you and spit out your bones," he growled.

"There's no need for eating or bone-spitting," Cloveris quipped.

The troll narrowed his eyes. "Oh, a joker, huh? I'll start with you, funny one, and maybe it will tickle my belly and I'll giggle with every bite." As the troll threatened, his voice rumbled like thunder.

Without hesitation, Cloveris raised his hand, muttering a spell under his breath. The troll's eyes widened as he spun in dizzying circles before collapsing onto the bridge with a mighty crash.

"Ha! You showed him!" Ralsky roared with laughter while Crumbzy chuckled alongside him.

Cloveris grinned. "I think my magic's improving!" He raised his hand to his diamond necklace, mumbling a few more words of gibberish, and then suddenly a soft glow enveloped Ralsky, Crumbzy, and Charmzy.

"What was that? I feel . . . lighter," Crumbzy said, hovering slightly above his horse. He laughed as a bottle of alchemical liquid materialized in his hand.

But their amusement was short-lived. The wooden planks beneath them began to creak just as the faint echo of ominous footsteps reached them. The bridge began swaying from side to side.

The four companions froze as tension gripped the air. Without warning, a troll emerged from the shadows under the bridge. His hulking figure towered over them, his greenish skin glistening in the moonlight.

Then a second troll appeared. He seemed to be the elder of the trolls, towering over his kin with a massive, weathered frame that seemed carved from ancient stone. His cracked, moss-covered skin hinted at his deep connection to the forest, while his amber eyes gleamed with wisdom beneath a heavy brow. A tangled beard of silver and earth-brown roots clung to his chest, adding to his air of solemn dignity.

Though fearsome in size, he moved with deliberate calm, his voice commanding respect and patience. Around his neck hung a rusted iron chain bearing an ancient stone medallion, symbolizing his role as guardian of troll-kind and protector of the old ways. Behind his hardened exterior lay a deep sense of duty and the quiet burden of guiding his people through these dark times.

Behind him, five more trolls appeared. And none looked pleased.

"What is this?" the greenish troll bellowed, peering down at his fallen brother. "What have you done to our Brutus?"

Brutus, the towering troll who had blocked their way, slowly shook off his daze and rose to his feet, rattling his head from side to side.

"What just happened?" he muttered, confusion evident in his expression. But as his vision cleared, his gaze locked onto Cloveris and rage flared in his eyes. "It was you!" he roared, charging toward Cloveris.

Then Ralsky tightened his fists and thrust them in the air, creating a mirror in front of Brutus who slammed into it and dropped back to the ground in a daze.

The elder troll shouted, "Stop this nonsense at once!"

Charmzy dismounted from his horse and approached the wise, older troll. "If I may make a proper introduction, I'm Charmzy, and these are my companions: Ralsky, Crumbzy, and Cloveris. We mean you no harm."

"Did I hear that right?" Gramal asked.

A tall and stout but smaller female troll with wavy hair standing high above his head chimed in, "Yes, Gramal, that's what he said—no harm." Her tone was slightly mocking.

Gramal's eyes narrowed as Charmzy stepped forward and said, "Gramal, you seem wise. We're only asking to cross the bridge peacefully. Please allow us to continue our journey. We don't want any more trouble."

Gramal, the wise troll, spoke in a deep and rumbling voice. "No trouble, you say. Yet you attack my family with this black magic from that green-haired boy and those pesky gnomes. It seems you are the trouble here. What's your name again?"

"The name is Charmzy."

The greenish troll roared and said, "You sound magically delicious." Then, the entire group of trolls laughed.

Charmzy remained calm. "My companions are Ralsky, Crumbzy, and Cloveris. We mean you no harm."

The older troll, who seemed to be their leader, squinted at Charmzy. "Did I hear that right?" he asked incredulously.

Before Charmzy could respond, the stout and wavy-haired troll stepped forward. "Yes, Gramal, you heard him right," she said. A hint of mockery lingered in her voice.

Charmzy seized on the moment. "We're simply trying to cross this bridge. If you could kindly allow us passage, we promise you no more trouble."

Gramal raised a hand to silence them, though amusement still flickered in his eyes. "We built this bridge with our bare hands, and everyone who crosses must pay the toll."

Charmzy paused, glancing back at his friends before leaning in. "I don't have money to give you," he admitted, showing Gramal his empty hands.

Gramal shifted his gaze to the horses. "Well, you've got horses. That'll do."

"The horses are not ours to give," Charmzy insisted. "We're on an important quest."

"Where are you headed?" Gramal asked, his curiosity piqued.

Ralsky and Crumbzy dismounted and came up beside Charmzy. "It's none of your business where we're headed!" Ralsky snapped, his temper flaring. "Let us pass with our horses, or else!"

Brutus loomed closer, sneering down at Ralsky. "Or what?"

"Or Cloveris will spin you like a ball of yarn!" Crumbzy blurted out. His remark earned a fresh round of troll laughter, some rolling on the bridge in hysterics.

"Alright, enough!" Gramal motioned for silence, his tone firm. Turning to Charmzy, he said, "We know about leprechauns coming for the Hemlock Rainbow. That's why we've constructed bridges to assist them in reaching their destination. However, everyone who has used our bridges has returned empty-handed or never returned to pay us with the gold. If you wish to use our bridge, you'll need to offer something in exchange before stepping onto it, as there's no guarantee of your return. Immediate payment is necessary, so the horses will do if you have no coins."

After some thought, Charmzy asked to speak with Gramal privately. "You seem like a troll of your word, Gramal. If I tell you something important, will you help me in exchange for something greater than coins?"

Gramal chuckled, "Let me guess, you're the chosen one of the Hemlock Rainbow?"

The serious look on Charmzy's face wiped the grin from Gramal's. "I am the chosen one. I need your help to reach the Hemlock Circle and confront the warlock and witch. If I fail, they will ruin these lands—including your home. But I cannot give you the horses. They belong to King Olaf."

Gramal's eyes widened. "King Olaf?" He stepped closer, and as he inspected the horses' collars, his gaze landed on the royal insignia. "These are indeed King Olaf's horses," he murmured, the name sparking memories. "He is a man of his word. If you carry his trust, then I believe you."

Gramal's stern expression softened. "Charmzy, we trolls are not just guardians of bridges—we protect these lands. Your mission affects us all. You have our support."

At Gramal's command, the trolls stepped aside, allowing Charmzy and his companions to pass. The elder troll's deep voice echoed, "We'll escort you safely to your destination. But for tonight, it's late. May we offer you shelter and food?"

In response, Crumbzy's stomach growled loudly, prompting the trolls to break into laughter. "I guess that's a yes," Charmzy said with a smile.

Crumbzy nodded eagerly. "Yes, please. I'm starving!"

Cloveris agreed. "Rest would benefit us before we reach Hemlock Circle."

Gramal gestured toward a hidden path. "Follow me." The trolls led them to a clearing with a roaring fire and soft beds made from moss and leaves. The savory scent of stew filled the air, making Crumbzy's stomach rumble louder.

As they ate, the trolls shared stories of the forest from before the Malrends, Warlock Winfred, and Witch Madison brought destruction. They spoke of past encounters with leprechauns and King Olaf. Their tales eased the tension as the night wore on. Charmzy, Cloveris, Ralsky, and Crumbzy savored a rare moment of peace, knowing they had earned the friendship of the trolls.

Thunderbolt circled above before landing next to Charmzy. "You deserve a rest, too," he murmured, stroking the hawk's feathers. Thunderbolt cooed softly, settling in by the fire.

As the night deepened, the group found comfort in the trolls' hospitality and renewed their resolve to face the challenges awaiting them at Hemlock Circle.

Chapter Twelve
The Awakening of Hemlock Circle

The following morning brought unexpected rainfall over Hemlock Woods—a rare sight in the dry, brown landscape. Creatures and trees emerged from hiding, eagerly drinking from the rain-soaked ground. Some even danced in the droplets, sensing that something miraculous was on the horizon.

The trees—Sherman, Cyrus, and Anne—whispered their message through the forest, calling all living beings to action. Today would be either a day of "Spring Bloom" or "Doom's Day." The trees warned that this was the final chance to push back against the darkness. The forest's fate rested on their decision to stand with the chosen one, Charmzy. If they did not fight, the devastation would be permanent. But if they united, they had a chance to restore what had once been a thriving, vibrant home. The choice was clear: they had to win.

As Charmzy and his companions prepared to depart for Hemlock Circle, they gathered their belongings and mounted their horses. The trolls promised to follow closely behind, rallying their forces and preparing their wagons for the battle that awaited them.

High above, Thunderbolt soared through the rain-soaked clouds, his heart heavy. He couldn't shake thoughts of Chelsea. Was she still loyal to Winfred and Madison? Could she be planning to fight against her former companions? Deep down, he hoped she would return to him, to Nordheimer Castle, where they could once again fight alongside King Olaf.

Chelsea, though, had already made her decision. She had flown directly to Nordheimer Castle, intent on helping Thunderbolt. Approaching the castle, she used her telepathy to demand an urgent meeting with King Olaf, revealing herself as Thunderbolt's former companion. The guards were stunned by her telepathic message but wasted no time. They rushed to inform the king that Thunderbolt was in grave danger.

The king, seated on his grand throne, agreed to the meeting. Chelsea, filled with determination, said in a steady but urgent tone, "King Olaf, Winfred and Madison plan to ambush Thunderbolt and his companions at Hemlock Circle. They will disguise themselves to avoid detection and trick their way into the rainbow's magic. If they succeed, they will turn the rainbow to indigo, unleashing the Malrend spirits. These spirits will destroy every forest in their path."

King Olaf's brow furrowed as he listened. "And Thunderbolt? Is he still loyal to me?" he asked, concern evident in his tone.

"Yes," Chelsea assured him. "But time is running out. You must help him—help them all. Winfred and Madison will stop at nothing to bend the magic of the rainbow to their will."

King Olaf stood, his hand gripping the hilt of his sword. Beside him, Jester Jack stood at attention. "Then we ride for Hemlock Circle," Olaf commanded. "Jack, ready the soldiers and summon my commanders. We must reach the rainbow before it's too late."

"Yes, Your Majesty!" Jack responded. Then he dashed out of the grand hall to alert the commanders and prepare for battle.

As Chelsea soared above Nordheimer Castle, she watched the soldiers preparing their horses as urgency filled the air. The rain had subsided, and sunlight began to pierce through the gray clouds revealing a rainbow. But something was wrong. The once vibrant colors were fading.

Red—the symbol of fire, protection, and strength—was gone.

Orange—representing creativity and innovation—had vanished. Yellow—the color of the sun, hope, and healing—had disappeared. Green—tied to nature and the growth of forests—was faint. Blue—the color of wisdom and calmness, oceans, rivers, and lakes—had been reduced to a thin stripe. Meanwhile, Indigo—the symbol of darkness, evil, and mysticism—was growing, along with Violet—representing spirits and magic.

Chelsea swooped down to King Olaf stationed in his chariot. "Look at the rainbow—the colors." she called out. "Indigo and Violet are spreading. Madison and Winfred are brewing their potions and calling on dark spirits to gain control of the rainbow."

King Olaf looked up, his face hardening at the sight of the altered rainbow. "To Hemlock Circle!" he shouted to his soldiers. With a slap to their horses' hinds, the army surged forward, charging through the gates of Nordheimer Castle and racing toward Hemlock Circle.

Meanwhile, as the four men, Charmzy, Ralsky, Crumbzy, and Cloveris, approached the Hemlock Circle, they felt a deep sense of fatigue taking over them. Their horses also lost all their strength and began to move very slowly, each one in a different direction, their riders too tired to notice.

As he neared the Circle, Charmzy came across a prism through which he saw his grandmother, Lucy. "Grandma!" Charmzy shouted. Then he heard her voice. "Charmzy, what are you doing in these woods? I told you there is no place for you in these woods," she said.

Just across to the north, Ralsky was entering a different prism. He saw his reflection in what looked like mirrors of himself. In one he was saying, "I want that gold!" Another mirror showed him saying, "I will betray the leprechaun." In the next mirror his image asserted, "It is my land, my gold. I will crush the leprechaun."

To the south, Crumbzy and his horse stumbled onto yet another prism that spoke in a self-pitying tone. "I'm so clumsy. I can't do anything right." In the next mirror was a reflection of Crumbzy slouched over in despair. He heard himself saying, "I'm tired of Ralsky pushing me around," and "I'm tired of this Charmzy. I want the gold for myself."

Then, to the east, Cloveris's horse led him into a prism where he saw the body of Charmzy's father lying motionless, a four-leaf clover next to him. "You failed Finn, and you will fail again," a voice from the mirror said. Cloveris felt sad and dispirited.

High above was Thunderbolt who circled lower to scan the forest below. He knew something was amiss when he saw all four horses going in different directions, so he swooped down to check it out.

As Thunderbolt landed, Brutus and the band of trolls emerged from the underbrush. They raised their weapons of jagged clubs made from enchanted stone, but their eyes were more calculating than hostile. When Thunderbolt told them that the four men and their horses had veered off course, the elder troll, Gramal, stepped forward, his face full of concern. "I've felt a disturbance in these woods. A dark force is pulling them apart."

Thunderbolt ruffled his feathers and flew to each of his four companions, the band of trolls following below. One glance from the sky revealed to Thunderbolt the confusion etched on their faces. Charmzy remained frozen, staring into the image of his grandmother in the prism. Ralsky was transfixed by his own reflection, while Crumbzy mumbled in frustration pacing in front of the shimmering mirrors. Cloveris stood with his head bowed, his gaze locked on the spectral image of Finn Cloverborn.

When the band of trolls reached Charmzy, Gramal stepped up and asserted, "This is no ordinary magic—it's Winfred and Madison's doing. They're forcing them to confront their worst fears and desires."

Understanding the urgency, Thunderbolt let out a screech.

"We must snap them out of it before it's too late," Gramal warned, gripping his enchanted club.

With swift movements, Thunderbolt darted toward Charmzy. He flapped his wings wildly, creating a gust that blew through the prism. The vision of Grandma Lucy flickered and then vanished, breaking the trance. Charmzy blinked, shaking his head as if waking from a dream. "Thunderbolt . . . what just happened?"

Gramal motioned for his trolls to disperse and dispel the trance that held the others captive as well. Brutus and two of his strongest trolls rushed toward Ralsky. They shattered the mirrors around him with their gleaming clubs. The twisted reflections in the mirrors splintered and disappeared. Ralsky gasped as if jolted out of a deep slumber, his anger replaced with clear-mindedness.

As the trolls worked to free Crumbzy from the bewitchment of the mirrors, Thunderbolt flew toward Cloveris. Following Thunderbolt, Gramal found Cloveris transfixed by the image of Finn. Gramal raised his hand, casting a faint glow over the prism. The vision of Finn disappeared and the dark magic that had trapped Cloveris was broken. Cloveris looked up, his face pale but resolute.

Gramal sighed, his expression grave. "This is just the beginning. Winfred and Madison will stop at nothing to break your bond and exploit your weaknesses. Don't let them succeed. The rainbow holds power for both good and evil, and if you let your doubts or fears take over, they'll win control of it."

Charmzy, who had made his way over in search of his friends, nodded and thanked Gramal. Gramal had more to say from his deep well of wisdom.

"You see, Charmzy, I wasn't always the elder troll you see before you today. There was a time when I was like any other—strong, fierce, proud of my tribe. We were the guardians of Hemlock Woods, protectors of the forest. That rainbow wasn't just a source of magic. It was life itself. We trolls understood its power and knew that it required us to look after it as well, to help keep the harmony."

He paused, his eyes darkening as memories resurfaced. "But then came Winfred and Madison. Back then, they weren't the monsters you know today. It was their uncle, Gideon Malrend, who was truly evil. He was the one who sought the power of the rainbow to corrupt it with black magic and seize control of both realms. He cared for Winfred and Madison but exposed them to the dark arts when they were still teenagers. At first, they rejected the darkness. They preferred their carefree days in the forest playing with their animals. But that wasn't Gideon's plan. He had no intention of letting them become a white witch and a good warlock."

Charmzy listened intently as Gramal continued.

"Everything changed when Gideon battled the Cloverborns for control of the rainbow. That was the day Winfred and Madison experienced the true power of the dark side. It began with a small nugget of magic their uncle stole during the fight against Ciaran. The power they tasted that day twisted into greed, poisoning their hearts. They began to crave more, wanting to bend it to their will. From that moment on, they no longer saw the rainbow as something to honor—they saw it as something to control."

Gramal leaned forward, his massive hands resting on his knees. "I led the first battle against them. My tribe and I—we fought with everything we had along with your grandfather Ciaran. But the warlock and the witch were clever, and their dark magic grew stronger with every passing day. As proud, noble, and strong as our trolls are, we couldn't stop corruption from spreading. The Malrend family poisoned the balance. I watched as my kin fell, one by one, either destroyed or turned by the dark magic."

His voice grew heavy with grief. "I lost many, but none hurt more than losing Elara, my mate. She was the heart of our tribe, a healer, a light in the darkness. When she fell, I knew the troll era—the great era—was over. Our tribe was scattered and broken. And I . . . I was left to bear the burden."

Charmzy shifted, sensing the deep sorrow behind Gramal's words.

With a long sigh, Gramal then said, "I retreated deep into the forest and dedicated my life to understanding the rainbow's true nature. It wasn't just magic. It was a delicate balance that bends to those who honor it, not to those who seek to control it. And that's when I realized . . . the rainbow would always lean towards balance. If the darkness grew too strong, it would take the light to regain that balance. If the light burned too bright, darkness would come to offset it."

Gramal locked his gaze on Charmzy, his expression grave. "That's where you come in, Charmzy. You're not just the chosen one because of your lineage. You're the chosen one because you have the capabilities to restore our forest and all of nature before the darkness overtakes all aspects of life on Earth and the celestial realms."

Charmzy stared down at his hands wondering if any magic would suddenly appear, like lightning bolts shooting out from his fingertips. His face held uncertainty as he answered, "I'm not sure if or how I can manifest these amazing capabilities."

Gramal said, "Charmzy, it will come from the heart. I know that you have it deep within you. You are a force unlike any guardian before you. I feel it in my soul."

Then Gramal looked out upon the group and said, "Listen, we must all find our special magical strength before the witch, Madison, corrupts the rainbow and turns it into full indigo. If Madison and Winfred succeed, the Malrend spirits will rise. Then the light will be gone forever and the world will fall into chaos."

He sighed, leaning back slightly. "The rainbow doesn't bend to force, Charmzy. It bends to honor. Your bloodline may have goodness and honor in it, but that means nothing if you don't understand what the rainbow truly needs. It needs selflessness. Now, it's up to you to restore what was lost."

Gramal's voice softened as he concluded. "Remember, this fight is for the very soul of Hemlock Rainbow which holds the world together."

"I . . . I never realized how deeply the rainbow's magic was intertwined with this world's balance," Charmzy said. His voice was quiet and filled with awe. "I thought it was just about stopping Winfred and Madison, but it's more than that, isn't it?"

He glanced up at the rainbow, now faint in the distance, its indigo hue a looming threat. "All this time, I've been focused on the battle ahead, but what you're saying is . . . this is about something much bigger. It's about protecting more than just a forest—it's about keeping the balance of the realms."

As he spoke these words, Charmzy stood a little taller, determination lighting his eyes. "I won't let the rainbow fall to darkness, Gramal."

Cloveris, who had been standing quietly beside Charmzy, stepped forward, his eyes glimmering with understanding.

"Charmzy," he began, his voice smooth and resonant. "I've watched you grow over the course of this journey. What Gramal said is true— the rainbow chooses those who honor it, not those who seek to possess it. But you . . . you've carried this burden with more grace than you realize."

Cloveris looked at the horizon, his long fingers tracing the air as if touching invisible strands of magic. "I may not have known your father for long, but I can see him in you. Not just his courage but his ability to inspire those around him. You've brought us all together, Charmzy—Ralsky, Crumbzy, the trolls, even Thunderbolt. None of this was by chance. The rainbow doesn't just choose. It also reveals. It shows who we are beneath our fears and doubts."

Turning back to Charmzy, Cloveris placed a hand on his shoulder. "Your father fought for the magic of this land, yes. But he also fought for the future, for you. And now, you're not just living in his shadow. You're carving your own path, one that will outshine any legacy."

Cloveris' expression softened, his normally stoic demeanor giving way to something Charmzy sensed as comforting. "You don't need to carry the weight alone. We're all here with you, and together we'll face whatever dark magic Winfred and Madison have planned. Trust yourself and trust the bond we've built. That's the real magic."

The wind stirred softly as though it were heeding Cloveris' words, weaving through the trees in quiet agreement.

In the distance, beyond the towering treetops, Chelsea soared high above leading the charge. Below her, King Olaf's army marched steadily through the forest. Unbeknownst to Charmzy and his companions, reinforcements were on their way—an army determined to rid the forest of the black magic that plagued it.

Chapter Thirteen
Indigo Rainbow

Back at Black Rock Castle, Chelsea's warning proved accurate. In the depths of their dark lair, Madison and Winfred stood before a massive cauldron, its surface bubbling and hissing with strange glowing liquids. Each ingredient they added was more sinister than the last—vials of silver mist, crushed bones of forgotten beasts, the venom of serpents, and the essence of shattered dreams. As the potions swirled together, dark tendrils of smoke rose from the cauldron, curling around the siblings like a living presence.

"This will do more than just confuse them," Madison whispered, her voice dripping with malice as she dropped a shard of obsidian into the brew. "It will trap them in their worst fears. Each prism will reflect their doubts, their darkest thoughts, turning their minds against themselves."

Winfred stirred the potion with his staff until the liquid inside turned a deep, unnatural indigo. "They'll see illusions of betrayal, failure, and fear—and they will be paralyzed by their insecurities. Charmzy and his companions will lose the will to fight and then the rainbow's power will be ours."

They added some final touches—a feather from a cursed raven, the blood of a fallen warrior, and a tear from the goddess of despair. The cauldron surged and the prisms began to form, shimmering and pulsating with dark energy. These magical traps would not just cloud the mind. They would weaken the spirit, forcing Charmzy and his allies to question their loyalty, strength, and even their very purpose.

They continued crafting more sinister potions, summoning dark spirits to aid them in battle. One such creation summoned shadow wolves—phantoms of the night that could strike swiftly, draining the life force of their enemies with a single bite, then vanishing into darkness before a counterattack. From above, they called upon razor-winged crows, their feathers sharp as blades and able to penetrate like arrows, while their piercing screeches disoriented and weakened anyone who heard them.

Winfred paused in his stirring, his staff hovering above the cauldron as his eyes drifted to the window and scanned the sky, searching.

"Why so grim, my brother?" Madison inquired, noticing the change in his mood.

"Where is my loyal Chelsea?" Winfred muttered with a hint of unease. What if she's been injured by our enemies!" Winfred winced at the thought of her being helpless and in the hands of his enemies.

"Or . . ." Madison teased, her voice laced with dark amusement as she continued stirring, "perhaps she has sided with the leprechaun and is planning an attack on us as we speak!"

"Do not say that!" Winfred snapped, though his tone held a hint of doubt. "Chelsea was the one who gave us the idea for the sneak attack, remember? She's loyal to me. Perhaps . . . we'll see her tonight." He returned his gaze to the sky when something caught his eye just as he was about to turn away.

With sudden enthusiasm, he exclaimed, "Look, my sister! The rainbow! The potions are working—the Indigo and Violet are spreading. We're almost there!"

In her excitement, Madison dropped her broom into the cauldron with a splash. "Oh, blast it!" she muttered, rushing to the window. But a grin spread across her face when she saw the growing darkness in the rainbow.

"Yes, Winfred, it's turning! We still have great powers and soon we will have more. Once Charmzy opens the rainbow, we can access the powerful talisman." Her voice brimmed with wicked glee. "We must hurry—finish these potions and get to Hemlock Circle in disguise. We'll position ourselves close enough to seize the rainbow's power the moment it opens!"

As the rainbow began to fade and the air grew damp, Charmzy and his companions neared their destination. Thunderbolt uttered a piercing cry that echoed above them, signaling they had arrived at Hemlock Circle.

Crumbzy and Ralsky glanced up at the golden eagle. "We must be very close," Crumbzy said. Gramal, ever vigilant, stepped forward. "Let me take the lead," the elder troll advised. "I know these woods well, and the witch and warlock are more cunning than you can imagine."

The four men dismounted from their horses, moving cautiously through a narrowing path of trees that seemed to guide them toward the hidden circle. Suddenly, an eerie sound echoed through the air, growing louder with each step. Gramal raised his hand, stopping them. "Do you hear that?" he asked, his voice low.

Cloveris nodded, eyes narrowing. "Yes. It's getting closer." Then, something strange happened—Cloveris' hands began to glow with a blue light while Ralsky's glowed red and Crumbzy's yellow. Gramal observed the phenomenon, his brow furrowing. "We're nearing the Hemlock Circle. Look—your energies are aligning with the colors of the rainbow."

Cloveris marveled at the surge of power in his body. "I've never felt anything like this."

Charmzy stared at his glowing companions in awe but felt nothing stir within himself. He remained still, troubled by the absence of power.

Suddenly, Thunderbolt let out a wild and raucous screech. The men looked up to see a swarm of crows circling the sky, their eyes locked on Thunderbolt. Then, in a storm of what seemed to be arrows, they unleashed upon the group their razor-tipped feathers.

"Take cover!" shouted Gramal.

Ralsky and Crumbzy exchanged glances. "We got this," they said in agreement. Crumbzy fumbled with his alchemy bottle and hurriedly mixed a potion. With a sudden pop, it exploded into glitter, covering them both in shimmering dust.

"What was that, Crumbzy?!" Ralsky yelled, exasperated.

"I was trying to make an invisibility potion! How was I supposed to know it'd turn into glitter?" Crumbzy said, brushing off the sparkles.

Ralsky rolled his eyes and shoved his foot into the ground. "We don't need invisibility—we need something solid!" As he raised his glowing hands, thick roots erupted from the ground, weaving into a protective wall against the falling arrows. "That should hold them off."

Crouched behind the barrier, they looked up to see the crows aiming their razor-like feathers at Thunderbolt, preparing to attack. But in an instant, the fierce cry of a hawk rang out. Chelsea dove toward Thunderbolt, feathers slicing through the air.

Behind them, King Olaf's army appeared, their steel-tipped spears flying upward toward the sky. Thunderbolt spotted Chelsea, then saw Olaf leading his soldiers, their arrows and spears cutting through the crows, each bird bursting into powder with every hit.

In a show of solidarity, Thunderbolt and Chelsea circled one another in a graceful aerial dance. Thunderbolt's heart swelled with emotion as he watched Chelsea swoop and strike the crows, turning them into powder with each swift blow. Below them, a menacing growl filled the air. It was a sound unmistakable to the trolls.

"It's the shadow wolves!" Brutus shouted, his voice tense with dread.

These were the legendary shadow wolves feared for their deadly bite. In a past battle, one of them had claimed Elara who was Brutus's mother and Gramal's beloved companion. The wolves moved in and out of the darkness, their red eyes glowing and sharp teeth flashing before they retreated into the shadows.

"Everyone, back-to-back!" Gramal commanded. Immediately the group formed a tight circle, their backs against one another.

Charmzy wanted to help, but he had yet to find his powers. He tightened his face, thinking hard about how he might harness his magic, but nothing came to him. Cloveris turned back to see Charmzy struggling and threw a spell toward his friend.

A moment later, Charmzy saw his father, Finn, standing in front of him, saying, "Charmzy, you got this. Listen to your heart and the magic will come." Charmzy placed one hand on his heart and felt a warmth overtake his very being. The next moment, he reached up for his hat and removed it. Fireworks emerged from the top of it, blasting into the sky and knocking out all the crows.

Cloveris stood frozen in awe of the magic Charmzy had just displayed. Then, Crumbzy, ever resourceful, pulled out a mini flask and started mixing ingredients. As he looked up at the shadow wolves, his hands trembled and some of the liquid spilled onto his fingers.

"Oh, I can do better than that!" Crumbzy exclaimed as he tossed the flask toward the barrier of roots Ralsky had conjured up.

Ralsky's eyes widened in alarm. "Wait, what are you—?"

The flask shattered on the roots and a puff of pink smoke erupted. To everyone's surprise, the roots began to writhe, twisting and curling like living creatures. What had once been a sturdy wall now moved erratically, confusing the shadow wolves as they approached.

Crumbzy grinned with pride. "See? Now they don't know where to step! It's like . . . a moving trap!"

Ralsky watched dumbfounded as the shadow wolves stepped into the shifting vines. The roots ensnared them, wrapping around their bodies until—poof!—they, too, exploded into powder. Ralsky rubbed his forehead and sighed. "Crumbzy, you're going to be the end of me. But . . . I guess that works," he admitted with reluctance.

Just then, Gramal signaled for the group to move. "To the Circle . . . quickly!" he urged, waving them forward. They rushed ahead, with King Olaf and his troops close behind. As they pushed through the last line of trees, they were met with a breathtaking sight. An ethereal glow surrounded a tree stump shaped like an angel in a flowing gown.

Charmzy was mesmerized by the intricate carvings on the tree stump. As his fingers traced the lines, he noticed the depictions of ancient battles—dragons clashing with witches, shadow wolves lunging at chariots, and armies of leprechauns and trolls with gleaming clubs upraised. Among them, to his astonishment, was a carving of himself, standing with Ralsky, Crumbzy, and Cloveris.

"It's us," Charmzy whispered, his voice filled with awe. "Look, Cloveris."

Cloveris knelt beside him, studying the carving. "You're right. This image . . . it's the four of us, etched into the tree."

Gramal furrowed his brow, clearly perplexed. "This is not possible," he muttered, moving closer to inspect the carving, his wise eyes scanning each detail.

As Charmzy brushed his hand across the carved face of the angel at the top of the stump, a bright, magnetic green light erupted from his body, casting a radiant glow over the Circle. Everyone instinctively stepped back, eyes wide with shock.

In the next instant, the ancient stump split down the middle, creaking as it slowly opened like a door, revealing a dazzling light within. The image of an angel projected into the sky shimmered and awakened a rainbow that began to form above them. But just as the rainbow began to appear, a large tree branch swung over the opening, blocking the emerging arc of colors. The surrounding trees shook violently, thrashing as if warning of something sinister. The men watched in disbelief as four massive trees swung their branches wildly at one another.

Then came a thunderous roar. "You will burn for this, you traitors!" Winfred's voice bellowed out from one of the trees. A tree twisted and warped, morphing into the menacing figure of the Warlock himself. Another tree shrank and contorted until it transformed into the petite but fierce witch Madison.

Olaf stepped forward, towering behind Charmzy and Cloveris, his eyes locked on the pair. "If it isn't the greedy warlock and the fiery witch," he said, his voice steady and commanding.

Winfred snorted, narrowing his eyes as he took in the Viking king. "So, you've returned, Olaf—ready for defeat a second time?" he said, his voice dripping with malice.

Madison's gaze shifted to Charmzy. "And who is this?" she asked, her tone laced with mockery. Winfred moved closer. "Are you the little leprechaun we're supposed to fear?" His jeering was soon joined by Madison's shrill cackling.

Winfred circled Charmzy, his eyes holding a questioning stare. "Look at you—barely more than a sprout, and yet here you stand, thinking you can challenge me," he sneered. "Do you understand the power you're meddling with? This is *MY* forest, *MY* dominion. The Hemlock Rainbow's magic belongs to *ME,* and *ME* alone—"

"Ahem!" Madison interrupted. Her gaze was as cold as ice.

Winfred flinched, then quickly corrected himself. "I meant to say *our* forest. Yes, of course—*our* forest. Madison's and mine."

Charmzy moved in closer to Winfred, taking an aggressive stance. "Listen here, you dreaded warlock. This forest belongs to every one of us. It belongs to the leprechauns, the gnomes, the creatures, the trees, the birds, and the bees. I will restore its beauty and stop you!"

Winfred paused and, leaning into Charmzy's ear, lowered his voice to a taunting whisper. "Do you know what happens to those who try to take what's mine? They are turned to ash—scorched and scattered to the winds."

He then straightened and swept his gaze over Charmzy's companions. "And that goes for anyone foolish enough to stand by your side . . . trolls, gnomes, birds, and whatever other pitiful creatures Olaf dragged in to aid you."

Ralsky clenched his fists as defiance burned in his eyes. "The only ones losing here will be you, Winfred—and your twisted sister."

Madison gasped, "How dare you call me twisted." She looked down at her neatly polished crimson fingernails and brushed them with a smile. Then, she held her fingers up high, rolled them in circles, and said, "I'll twist you!" As she pointed towards Ralsky, twisting and turning her hand, he gripped his stomach and fell over in pain. Madison was twisting something inside his very belly.

Winfred and Madison laughed as Ralsky slid to the floor in agony. Then, as they continued to watch Ralsky writhe in pain, Winfred smiled and let out a low mocking sneer. Crumbzy ran to his cousin and lifted him up as Madison slowly released her twisting spell.

Charmzy, trembling with a mix of distress and curiosity, broke through the chaos and demanded, "What did you do to my father?" Winfred's snide smile vanished, replaced by a calculating stare and restrained anger.

Before Winfred could respond, Cloveris placed a gentle but firm hand on Charmzy's shoulder. "Don't let him provoke you, Charmzy. Focus on what you must do. Listen to your inner self and find the magic inside."

Charmzy hesitated, torn between his need for answers and the urgency of the situation. With a deep sigh, he nodded, forcing aside his grief and rage. Cloveris was right, there was more at stake than vengeance. If he let his emotions take over, Winfred would turn the rainbow's magic into darkness and all the realms would go dark.

Madison taunted Charmzy. "Oh, Finn . . . little old Finn. What did happen to that foolish man?" She tapped a finger on her chin, a wicked glimmer in her eyes. "Ah, yes!" She snapped her fingers. "Brother, wasn't it that Cloverborn man who tried to strip you of your magic?"

Winfred's grin widened as his gaze locked onto Charmzy. "Oh, why yes! Indeed, my sister! Your father was a stubborn fool, Charmzy. He thought he could strip me of my power but instead he made me stronger. He led me straight to the rainbow and helped me unleash Ciaran—the guardian who defied the realm's rules."

His smile twisted into a sneer. "Are you here to learn the tragic truth about your grandfather and father? Or shall we move on to claiming our rainbow?"

He leaned closer, his voice dropping to a scornful whisper. "Though I enjoy a good battle, I much prefer breaking your spirit, piece by piece, with every secret I know."

Madison's smile sharpened. "Oh, look, it's Grandpa Troll—Ciaran's dear friend. The one who left him behind when he needed help the most."

"That's a lie!" Gramal roared, his eyes blazing. "You ambushed us! I lost Elara that day . . . I was there, in the battle, searching for Ciaran. Even after the battle, when he did not return to Dalkey, I continued searching for him."

Madison's laughter rang out, sharp and cruel. "Oh, poor clueless Gramal," she cooed mockingly. "Do you want to know what really happened to the 'Protector of the Hemlock Rainbow?' How did the mighty guardian fall so low?"

Charmzy tightened his jaw, but he couldn't hide the flicker of curiosity in his eyes. "Whatever you have to say, I don't believe your lies!" Charmzy said.

"I have no reason to lie," Madison purred.

"What did you do to my grandfather?" Charmzy demanded as anger rose in his voice.

Madison shook her head slowly, her expression almost pitying.

"Me? Oh no, Ciaran's fall was his own doing. He was chosen to guard the rainbow—sworn to protect its magic and uphold its balance. But Ciaran . . ." She leaned closer, dropping her voice to a conspiratorial whisper. "Ciaran wanted more."

She stepped back, savoring the shock on Charmzy's face. "He found something hidden deep within the rainbow's core. It was an ancient talisman, a power no guardian was ever meant to touch, a magic capable of amplifying one's strength tenfold. And what did he do? He tried to seal it off, to control it, thinking he could keep it safe from dark forces like us."

She continued, a smirky smile spreading across her face. "But in doing so, he broke the realm's first and most sacred rule: Guardians must never wield more of the rainbow's power than they're granted. He tried to use it to create a permanent barrier—to lock away the dark spirits from the human world and bind them forever on the other side of the rainbow."

Charmzy's eyes widened as the horror of what she was saying dawned on him. "The Celestial Realm . . . he was trying to—"

"Oh, so you've heard of it, have you?" Madison interrupted in a mocking tone. "Yes, the Celestial Realm—the place where good spirits and magical beings are supposed to reside. The rainbow was meant to bridge the two worlds in perfect harmony. But Ciaran—" she spat his name, "thought he could play savior and fix it on his own."

She gestured theatrically at the twisted forest around them. "He thought the darkness was spreading too quickly, tainting the rainbow's essence. So, in a desperate move, he tried to seal the bridge, trapping the good spirits inside to 'protect' them. But in doing so, he made it worse, locking them away along with his now corrupted dark spirit. But we still had the upper hand in the human world. So, in essence, he left it, unknowingly, unlocked to us."

Madison's smile widened. "That's when the rainbow split and the talisman clung to his chest. The light—nature's guardians, the essence of all that is pure—was caged on the other side, helpless, while here, in the human realm, the dark magic was left exposed—a gateway for us to gain more power."

She leaned in closer, her voice dropping to a menacing murmur. "Ciaran thought he was saving everyone by sacrificing himself."

Winfred stepped forward, his voice dripping with satisfaction. "Without the balance, Madison and I began using the fragments of power your father, Finn, mistakenly unlocked for us when he came looking for your grandfather. And do you know who became the gatekeeper of this broken, corrupted magic?"

Charmzy swallowed hard. "Ciaran . . ."

Winfred's smile was wicked and triumphant. "Yes, little leprechaun. Ciaran, the so-called 'Protector,' became its Dark Guardian. When your father Finn unlocked the rainbow, he realized what his father had done. He tried to seal us out of the rainbow forever along with Ciaran and the magical talisman stone. But instead, he met his fate at my hands just before the barrier closed."

Charmzy stood straighter, anger flaring in his eyes. "It was you! You murdered my father—you stopped his heart!"

"Oh, that's where you're wrong," Winfred sneered. "Finn's body was a mere illusion I created to make you pesky leprechauns believe the Cloverborn line was dead. But had I known he had a son, well, I would have gotten rid of you a long time ago."

Charmzy clenched his fists as the full weight of the revelation hit him. "Then where is he? Where is my father?"

"Trapped on the other side of the rainbow," Winfred replied coolly. "Well, just before the rainbow was sealed off, I placed a spell on your father. I'm sure his fate was the same as Ciaran's, with no way out. The two of them will remain for eternity in agony, bound as guardians of the very darkness they sought to lock away."

"And the good spirits?" Charmzy's voice was strained. "The ones trapped on the other side?"

Madison's smile turned mocking, her eyes feigning sympathy. "They're still there, waiting and hoping for someone to save them. But they grow weaker with every inch of the rainbow that turns to indigo, because they have been in battle with Ciaran trying to restrain his dark magic."

She spread her arms wide, gesturing at the corrupted landscape around them. "So, you see, dear Charmzy, your precious rainbow is already ours. Ciaran couldn't protect it, and you . . ."—she pointed at him, her smile darkening—"you will fail just like your father and your grandfather." Madison leaned closer. "Unless, of course, you decide to bend its magic, too. Maybe you'll be the one to set them free. Or maybe . . ." she trailed off with a sparkle in her eyes, "you'll trap yourself—just like they did." She flipped her hair back in laughter.

Winfred chimed in and pointed to the sky. "Charmzy, do you see the indigo and violet spreading in the sky? That's Ciaran's agony twisting the colors darker every day. And every time I tap into the rainbow's power," he added with a sneer, "I hear his screams—his defiance, his pleas. But there's no one left to save him . . . except you."

Charmzy listened with a heavy heart to the disclosure that his grandfather was suffering in the rainbow and his father was somewhere lost in the midst of ethereal beings. His friends and allies were saddened as well.

Winfred and Madison, though, looked at the group with glee and satisfaction on their faces.

"Are you ready to meet your grandfather, Charmzy? Are you willing to become part of the very force that destroyed your family?" Winfred asked.

Charmzy could feel his heart pounding. The idea of his family suffering—his grandmother and mother losing their husbands, his grandfather and father trapped in a corrupted form within the rainbow all of these years--shattered something inside Charmzy. Yet, a flicker of determination began to grow within him.

"I'll free them!" he said, his voice trembling but fierce.

"You will, and we will help you," Cloveris assured him.

The smile on Winfred's face faltered, but only for a moment. "Brave words. But bravery won't be enough. If you want to save them, you must face Ciaran first. And let me tell you—he's not the Ciaran you remember."

Madison's eyes sparkled with malice. "Are you ready to confront the shadow of your own bloodline, Charmzy? Are you ready to battle your grandfather—the Dark Guardian of the Rainbow?"

Chapter Fourteen
The Dark Guardian's Curse

Charmzy clenched his fists, his gaze darting from Winfred's mocking grin to Madison's cruel smirk. For a moment, he felt a wave of uncertainty wash over him. What could he possibly do against these two forces of evil, especially if his own grandfather, a guardian of the rainbow, had been corrupted and overtaken by darkness?

But then he heard Cloveris' voice echoing softly in his mind: "Listen to your inner self. The magic will come." Charmzy also recalled his father's words. "You are the Guardian of Hemlock Rainbow. All its power and treasures are yours to protect. If anything happens to me, you must find the angel and the rainbow and stand against the Malrend family. Protect life. It's your duty, my son. I love you, Charmzy,"

Taking a deep breath, Charmzy tried to push the taunts of Madison and Winfred out of his mind. "If Ciaran's truly trapped inside the rainbow, I'll get him and my father out. I won't let you manipulate his pain against me," Charmzy said.

Winfred's grin widened as he raised his hand. The air around the stump shone. "Ah, but you see little leprechaun, you don't have a choice now that you have unlocked the passageway to the rainbow. I've already called to the Dark Guardian. He's coming for you."

Suddenly, the ethereal light inside the tree stump shifted and darkened, and the rainbow poured out of the stump, crossing over the forest. The once-brilliant colors of the rainbow began to spiral and bleed thin like oil spreading in water. Shades of violet and indigo crept in, darkening the other colors of the rainbow. The image of the angel on the tree stump seemed to break into ripples, distorting into something surreal.

A low growl reverberated through the rainbow. Charmzy's heart thumped when a figure materialized within its darkened form.

He gestured for all his friends to stand back, emphasizing that this was his grandfather. Ralsky, Crumbzy, Cloveris, King Olaf, and the trolls obediently positioned themselves at a safe distance, observing as the dramatic confrontation unfolded before their eyes.

The figure at the entrance of the rainbow was tall and imposing, shrouded in a faintly glowing mist. Slowly, it took shape—a silhouette of a man with broad shoulders, draped in a cloak woven from shadows, and an indigo stone pulsing ominously in the center of his chest. But where Ciaran's face should have been, there was only darkness, and his eyes . . . his eyes glowed with an eerie, haunting light.

The shadow figure moved, its body shuddering as if struggling against invisible chains. For an instant, the darkness wavered and a faint and distant voice echoed from within.

"Charmzy . . .?" It was deep and filled with confusion and anguish.

Charmzy felt his chest tighten even while hope flickered in his eyes. "Yes, it's me! I'm here to help you! Just—just fight it! I know you're still in there."

But before he could say more, Winfred's laughter cut through the air. "You think words will save him? Foolish boy." He flicked his wrist and the shadow figure jerked violently, the indigo in its eyes flaring brighter.

"Prepare yourself, little one," Madison purred, her gaze as sharp as daggers. "Your beloved grandfather is about to tear you apart."

The shadow guardian lunged forward, raising an arm that merged into a massive blade of dark energy. Charmzy stumbled back, his heart pounding. He had no idea how to fight his own blood, especially when every fiber of his being screamed that he needed to save him, not destroy him.

"Don't just stand there!" Gramal bellowed, and then he ran in front of Charmzy to protect him. When the blade came crashing down, Gramal's stone club met it with a resounding clang.

"Use the rainbow's light, Charmzy! Call it to you—use its power against the darkness!" Cloveris yelled.

"But how?" Charmzy shouted, panic rising. "I don't—"

"You are the chosen one!" Cloveris called, his voice cutting through the chaos. "You don't have to understand it yet—just believe it! Feel it!"

Charmzy reached out with trembling hands towards the rainbow's light spilling out of the split tree. He closed his eyes, trying to drown out Winfred's taunts and the sound of Gramal straining against the shadowy attacks.

He focused on the true colors—red, orange, yellow, green, and blue. He pictured each hue as it should be, shining brightly and purely. Slowly, he began to feel something stir within him—a warmth, a tingling sensation that spread from his fingertips to his very core.

Charmzy snapped his eyes open. As he thrust his hand forward, a burst of vibrant emerald energy erupted from his palm, striking the shadow figure. The guardian reeled back, its dark form flickering.

"Grandfather! I know you're still there!" Charmzy cried, pouring everything he had into the beam of light. "I won't let Winfred and Madison twist you like this. Fight it! Fight them!"

For a moment, the shadow guardian hesitated. The blade of darkness in its hand wavered and the indigo glow in its eyes dimmed ever so slightly.

"Charmzy . . ." The voice was clearer this time, tinged with sorrow and recognition.

"Yes!" Charmzy shouted, his heart soaring. "Hold on, I'll free you, I—"

But before he could finish, a blast of dark energy struck him from the side, knocking him to the ground. Charmzy gasped in pain, his concentration shattered. The green light faded from his hand and the shadow figure roared, its form solidifying once more.

The Dark Guardian looked down upon Charmzy, seemingly puzzled at what he had done.

"Enough of this sentiment!" Winfred spat, and when he raised his hand, tendrils of eerie shadows writhed around his fingers. "You will obey, Ciaran, or I will rip your dark essence apart and remake you entirely!"

"No!" Charmzy struggled to rise, his vision swimming. "Leave him alone!" he shouted.

But Winfred just smiled, a cold, triumphant look in his eyes. "You'll have to do more than beg, little leprechaun."

Then the Cloveis and the gnomes began to use their powers to throw magical spells on Madison and Winfred, to distract them from interfering and give Charmzy a chance to recover.

Cloveris summoned a shimmering wall of light that momentarily blinded the witch, while Crumbzy and Ralsky mettered incatations as they tossed acorns that exploded into puffs of thick, iridescent smoke, obscuring the warlock's vision. "Ha! Bet you didn't see that coming!" Crumbzy shouted. Winfred turned towards the three men and began to chant a dark spell when Ralsky lifted his hands forward at the witch and warlock, conjuring a sudden gust of wind that knocked the warlock and the witch to the ground.

As Charmzy struggled to his feet, breathing hard, he knew he was out of time. He had to find a way to reach Ciaran—to break through the darkness holding him captive. But how? How could he fight something that was woven into the very magic of the rainbow itself?

"Listen to me, Charmzy!" It was the voice of his father, sounding strained. "The rainbow's power is yours. Reach for it—not just with your hands, but with your heart. You can't force it. You must trust it. Let it feel your intent."

Charmzy gazed back at the faint colors of the rainbow struggling beneath the shadows. He took a deep breath and felt his fear giving way. Once more, he raised his hand, but this time he didn't try to summon the magic.

He simply . . . asked. "Help me. Please. Help me save my family."

And then, to his amazement, the colors began to respond. Red and orange flared to life followed by yellow, green, and blue. The rainbow's light surged through the stump, spilling over the clearing like a radiant wave. Charmzy felt it fill him with something deep and serene inside.

Winfred raised his staff to counter the light, but it was too late. Charmzy focused all his will, all his love and hope into the colors.

The shadow guardian stumbled, its form wavering. "Charmzy . . .?" Ciaran's voice was louder now, more solid.

"Yes! It's me! I'm here, Grandfather!"

The elder leprechaun, Ciaran, appeared as a twisted version of his former self—part shadow, part memory of the man he used to be—bound by darkness and trapped by the magical stone he once sought to control.

"Stay back!" the Dark Guardian growled, his voice deep and strained. "The stone's power has taken root in me. I am no longer the guardian I once was."

"You tried to protect us, Grandfather, but it's my turn now. I'll restore the rainbow. I'll free you," Charmzy said. He raised his palms, now flickering with the colors of the rainbow, and aimed them toward the Dark Guardian. Then, in a brilliant flash, the colors of the rainbow exploded, knocking the Dark Guardian to the ground. A light washed over the shadow and began purging the darkness inch by inch.

Finally, with one last shudder, the shadow guardian collapsed and the indigo faded from his eyes. The heavy chains on Ciaran shattered, and the magical talisman embedded in his chest—a brilliant, pulsating gemstone—lifted off of him.

Ciaran's true form emerged as an elder, both wise and powerful, his eyes clear and bright once more.

"Charmzy . . . my brave boy." His voice softened and filled with pride. "You've done it. You've broken the curse and restored me." The stone—the source of his corruption—floated into Charmzy's hand.

A mix of shock and fury twisted Madison's delicate features. "No, this isn't possible!" she hissed, taking a step back. "He should be under our control—bound to the darkness!"

Winfred's face contorted with rage and his fingers twitched as dark energy crackled around them. "It's impossible!" he bellowed, thrusting his staff toward Ciaran. "Darkness turned you, and I will bind you again!"

In a deep and commanding tone, his chest pulsating with a fierce and radiant light, Ciaran said, "I swore to protect the rainbow's essence. And now that my grandson has freed me . . ."—his voice reverberated through the clearing, causing the ground to tremble—"you will pay for the corruption you've sown."

Ciaran swept his hand in a broad arc, releasing a surge of power. A burst of shimmering energy erupted from his palm, exploding in a wave of blinding light. Madison and Winfred shrieked as the force slammed into them, sending them hurtling backward.

"No!" Madison screamed, her body still flickering as she struggled to regain her balance. "You will obey, Ciaran! You belong to us!"

But the light held, pushing them further back until they were thrown clear of the rainbow's entrance. Their dark magic dissipated around them in tattered wisps.

"Go, Charmzy!" Ciaran shouted. He fixed his eyes on the evil siblings as they tried to rally their strength. "The talisman must be returned to the center of the rainbow before they recover and call upon the Malrend spirits, or the stone changes you, Charmzy!"

Ciaran then placed his hand on Charmzy's shoulder and transferred a surge of pure and uncorrupted power as a final gift to his grandson. "Take this strength, Charmzy," he said. "It is the power of every guardian before me and the knowledge of how to unlock the Celestial Realm."

"I'll use it wisely, Grandfather," Charmzy whispered. "I'll save them all."

As Ciaran's spirit started to dissipate, his face softened into a peaceful smile. "Lucy has been waiting for me. It's time for us to be together again." His form dissolved into a shimmering mist, rising to the heavens where a faint figure of Lucy appeared, welcoming him. Charmzy watched along with his friends, knowing his grandfather was finally at peace.

Cloveris lost no time reminding his friend of the urgent task at hand. "Hurry, Charmzy. Enter the rainbow and place the talisman back in the core of the rainbow."

Gramal followed suit. "Yes, hurry. I can feel the Malrend spirits coming near. Go now."

Holding the talisman, Charmzy felt its immense power surging through him with the promise of magical gifts vast and all-encompassing. He glowed with every color in the spectrum—but the rainbow remained shadowed. He knew he could not keep the talisman and its tremendous power for himself, or it would corrupt him too.

Charmzy rushed to the center of the rainbow where the barrier separating the Celestial Realm shimmered faintly.

"Hold the line! Protect the rainbow at all costs! Charmzy needs time." Gramal shouted. Another cry from their elder rallied the trolls to stand guard at the entrance to the rainbow.

Madison and Winfred soon recovered from Ciaran's attack. Their desperation growing, they decided to summon the Malrend spirits in an all-or-nothing gamble. Madison's shriek cut through the air as she and Winfred, still chafing from Ciaran's blow, chanted in unison, summoning the Malrend spirits from deep within the earth.

The Malrend spirits, in answer to the call, materialized out of nowhere, their claws reaching for the trolls. Gramal and his kin backed away from the rainbow as they fought fiercely, swinging their clubs with precision. Gramal batted away a large dark spirit as it tried to wrap itself around Brutus. "Back, you fiend!" he snarled. "You will not take our home!"

As he gracefully moved into position, King Olaf pulled his golden double-sided axe from his back. With his soldiers by his side, he slashed at the Malrend spirits. Each powerful swing of his enchanted weapon slashed and scattered the spirits into useless specks of dust.

Madison and Winfred flew past the fighting into the rainbow. Their faces twisted with rage as their eyes locked on the glowing talisman Charmzy held in his palm.

"You think you can win?" Winfred sneered.

"It's ours!" Madison shrieked, lunging toward him. "The power belongs to us!"

"You'll have to take it from me," Charmzy said in a steady voice. He continued to run along the rainbow, which seemed to go on forever. Then, when he saw the talisman brighten, he tossed it high into the air. All eyes followed as it arced gracefully and landed precisely at the core of the rainbow.

The warlock and the witch let out a loud cry as they watched the talisman return to its rightful position within the rainbow. Winfred raised his staff and Madison circled her wrist. Dark energy gathered around them as they conjured a spell for yet another assault on Charmzy.

But Charmzy, now glowing with the rainbow's full strength and his grandfather's power, thrust his hand forward, releasing a wave of radiant green energy. The energy erupted, bursting into gigantic four-leaf clovers that pushed Madison and Winfred backward, expelling them from the heart of the rainbow. He and Madison had no choice but to make their way back toward the entrance. As he left, Winfred yelled out in defiance that he would one day return to take back his power.

In the meantime, Charmzy made his way to the gleaming door behind which the ethereal spirits had been held captive. As he was about to place his glowing hand upon the door to release them, he heard an unfamiliar sound below the rainbow and sensed an uncomfortable heat slowly rising to envelop him.

Chapter Fifteen
The Rainbow's Restoration

Chelsea, the red-tailed hawk, soared above, her keen eyes scanning the battlefield. With a fierce cry, she turned to Thunderbolt whose golden feathers glinted in the light. "You must lead the aerial attack! Don't let any dark spirits reach Charmzy."

Thunderbolt nodded, his wings beating forcefully as he took to the skies. He let out a mighty cry, rallying the birds of the forest. Owls, hawks, and even sparrows joined the charge, diving at the shadowy forms that emerged from the power of dark magic and disrupting their advance. Ralsky and Crumbzy exchanged determined glances as they faced off against a horde of shadow wolves racing toward the rainbow's center.

"Let's show these mutts what we're made of," Ralsky muttered, his hands glowing red.

"Right behind you!" Crumbzy grinned, pulling out a series of tiny bottles. He flung them at the ground in front of the wolves, and with a pop, long thick vines erupted, twisting and tangling around the wolves' legs. As they struggled, Ralsky raised his hands and the vines burst into flames, sending the wolves howling and scattering back into the shadows.

"Nice work, Crumbzy," Ralsky said, giving his cousin a nod of appreciation.

Crumbzy shrugged, a mischievous grin on his face. "Can't let you have all the fun, can I?"

But the battlefield shifted again. As Winfred and Madison approached, dark energy hissed around them, and they began to chant spells out loud in unity. The sky turned black and from the shadows ghostly figures emerged—the Malrend spirits, their ethereal forms continuing to multiply. They hovered in the air, while others flew low on the forest ground wailing in haunting tones as they advanced toward Charmzy's friends.

The air turned to a crisp winter frost as a fog spread through the woods. Through the haze, Winfred and Madison arrived, their eyes burning like fire, their chests heaving with anger. Their dark magic swirled around them like a hurricane, thick and oppressive, distorting the light of the rainbow where the indigo had been receding and where red and yellow had begun to emerge.

King Olaf looked at the sky and witnessed the changes in color. He stood beside his troops and stepped forward with his axe raised high. "Hold your ground!" he roared, his voice carrying over the battlefield. "We will protect this place with everything we have!"

Gramal stepped forward, his gaze fierce as he raised his club high. "Trolls, to me!" he bellowed.

His kin—the mighty trolls of Hemlock—roared in response. Standing above the others, Brutus led the charge with a massive war club made from enchanted stone. "For the Hemlock Woods!" he cried, his voice booming across the battlefield.

The trolls surged forward, swinging their heavy clubs and scattering the Malrend spirits. But for every spirit that was struck down, two more appeared, their ghostly forms swirling around the trolls, whispering words of despair and doubt.

"We can't keep this up forever, Gramal!" Brutus called, smashing another spirit to mist.

As the trolls battled the spirits, King Olaf's army advanced, forming a protective ring around Charmzy's companions. Arrows flew and spears clashed against the shadowy forms that emerged from the ground.

"Brace yourselves!" King Olaf ordered. His axe flashed as he cut through a spirit trying to flank the line. "We must not let them reach the rainbow!"

But Winfred and Madison weren't finished yet. Seeing their spirits held at bay, they turned their attention back to the rainbow, their eyes blazing with fury.

"Enough games," Winfred snarled.

He lifted his staff high and the earth beneath them quaked violently. With a deafening roar, his form twisted and expanded, transforming into a massive red dragon. Flames burst from his jaws in scorching waves, forcing King Olaf and his men to stagger back, shields raised against the inferno.

Meanwhile, Charmzy's hand hovered an inch from the glowing door which pulsed beneath his fingertips. He felt its pull as the energy bouncing off the light on the door buzzed through his veins. This was the moment he had been waiting for. Angel Christel and his father Finn must be waiting behind this door. Charmzy focused his mind on getting the door opened and releasing the ancient forces that could turn the tide of the entire battle. He just had to find the strength to open it and the ethereal spirits would be free again.

Charmzy laid his hand upon the door and closed his eyes in concentration. Suddenly, a violent tremor shook the rainbow, nearly knocking him off his feet. He looked up, his heart hammering in his chest. A crash sounded from below the rainbow followed by a deafening roar. It was Winfred's face on the body of a dragon.

Charmzy's breath quickened. "No, no, no—not now!" He pressed his hand harder against the door, the light glowing brighter just beneath, but his concentration wavered.

Seconds later, another explosion rocked the rainbow. This time it came from outside the rainbow, from the forest where he heard his friends screaming and panicking. He pulled his hand away from the door. "I'll be back. I must help my friends," he whispered. Then, just as he about to turn around to exit the rainbow, the light brightened and the locks on the door swung open.

Charmzy lost no time. He sprinted out of the rainbow where he saw Winfred shaped into a dragon with fire sparking from his mouth like a lighter and Madison with a storm circling around her.

"You can't win this, Winfred!" Charmzy shouted. "The rainbow's power isn't meant for darkness. It's meant for balance."

"Balance?" Madison sneered, her magic swirling in agitation. "We don't want balance—we want dominion!"

With a flick of her wrist, she summoned a dark, writhing mass of energy that shot toward Charmzy followed by Winfred's fiery dragon breath. But before it could reach him, a shimmering barrier of ice appeared, blocking the attack.

"You'll have to get through me first," Cloveris said, his breath visible in the sudden chill.

"Why, look at what we have here! If it isn't a clover seedling that sprouted into a young man. I thought you were all dead!" Madison spat. "Do you think you can stop us now?"

"Yes," Cloveris replied. "And not just me—look around."

As he spoke, the battlefield lit up with a myriad of colors as the good spirits, now freed from the Celestial Realm, joined the fight. Beams of light shot down from the sky, striking at the dark creatures that swarmed the battlefield. The ground shook as the trolls, led by Gramal and Brutus, charged forward, their massive clubs swinging through the air, sending shadow wolves and dark spirits flying.

"We stand together!" Brutus roared.

But still they fought. Winfred spit fire onto the trees that tried to entangle him and Madison in their branches, while Cloveris shot out ice to guard the trees from catching on fire.

Madison and Winfred pressed closer to the rainbow's entrance. Charmzy stood tall, guarding the rainbow as Madison lunged toward him and the dragon released his hot breath. They lashed out like twin serpents. Charmzy raised his hands and a brilliant shield of light formed in front of him. But the force of their attack was immense, with Winfred's dragon flames and Madison's tornado swirl pounding against Charmzy's shield. Charmzy began to stagger back, his breath coming in heavy gasps.

"We will have that stone, boy!" Winfred snarled, pushing against the shield with everything he had. "You cannot stand against us!"

"You're wrong," Charmzy whispered, his eyes blazing with determination. "I'm not alone."

At that moment, his hand pulsed with power, and from the rainbow just behind Charmzy, a figure began to materialize. It was Finn—Charmzy's father—his body shimmering with the brightest light. The dragon and the witch froze. Charmzy turned around.

"Father?" Charmzy exclaimed, his voice choked with emotion.

"Charmzy, my son." Finn smiled gently. "You've done it. You've freed us."

He turned his gaze on Winfred and Madison, his expression hardening. "But there's still a fight to finish."

"NO!" Madison screamed as her face contorted with fury. "You're supposed to be dead from the dark hands of your father, Ciaran! You're supposed to be gone forever!"

Finn shook his head. "As long as the rainbow exists, there will always be hope."

With a flash of light, he joined Charmzy, their combined power forming a wave of pure, blinding magic. Winfred and Madison shrieked as the green light washed over them, their dark magic unraveling in its wake.

"NO!" Winfred transformed back into his warlock body and Madison bellowed within the swirls of her own tornado. Their forms flickered as the magic tore through them and a steel cage confined them.

"This isn't over! You can't—" the siblings yelled out from their cage.

Charmzy turned to Finn. "Why isn't it working? The rainbow still is not restored. We have returned the talisman, the spirits are free, and yet the rainbow still has more indigo—something's still missing!"

Finn looked at Charmzy, his eyes softening. "Balance, Charmzy, is not just about defeating evil. It's about harmony—about every color shining in its own way. Your friends . . . they must reflect the true colors of the rainbow."

It was then that Charmzy understood that each person represents a piece of the rainbow. Their desires and intentions are tied to their true colors, while the indigo and violet are overpowering because the others are rooted in self-interest.

As Charmzy faced his friends—King Olaf, Ralsky, Crumbzy,

Thunderbolt, Cloveris, Chelsea, and even Gramal—he realized what must be done.

"Everyone, listen to me! The rainbow isn't just about power or magic—it's about us, about the friendship and trust we've built. We're each a part of it. But we're out of balance because we're still holding on to what we want for ourselves."

His gaze turned to each of them. "Ralsky and Crumbzy, you sought gold. King Olaf, you wanted magic. Chelsea, you struggled with loyalty. Thunderbolt, you've always fought to prove yourself. But we have to let that go. If we want to save everything, we need to give our strengths freely and selflessly."

One by one, Charmzy's companions stepped forward and expressed a willingness to sacrifice their desires. Ralsky and Crumbzy came forward first. Crumbzy tossed his alchemical gold powder into the rainbow's core while Ralsky placed his cherished "lucky" gold coin into the swirling light.

"We always thought gold would solve everything, but it's never been about that," Ralsky said, his voice steady. "What's gold without the friends we've made?"

King Olaf stood tall, a look of resolve crossing his face. He drew his enchanted axe, the source of his magical power, and offered it to the rainbow. "I thought I needed more power to rule wisely, but real strength isn't in magic—it's in the people who stand by your side."

Thunderbolt landed softly beside Charmzy, bowing his head. "All I wanted was to show my strength, to prove myself as more than just a companion. But I see now—my loyalty is my strength." He opened his wings, channeling a protective, calming energy into the rainbow.

Chelsea hesitated but stepped forward as well. "I was lost in choosing sides. But I know now where my heart belongs—with those who fight for light, not control." She let out a soft hawk cry, sending a pulse of pure, guiding light into the core.

Gramal pulled out a relic from his past—a carved pendant of Elara, his beloved. "This is all I have left of her, but I'll give it up if it means saving what she fought for."

Cloveris conjured up the essence of his own magical glow of deep green. "As the keeper of the forests and rainbow, I thought I had to protect my power, the power of the Clovers. But power, unshared, is nothing." He let the green glow disperse into the rainbow.

As each friend placed their offering and intention into the rainbow, the colors begin to shift. The overpowering indigo and violet receded, blending harmoniously with the reds, oranges, yellows, greens, and blues. The sun rose, the rivers that ran dry were once again full of fresh water, the trees changed from brown to green, and the animals with their families by their sides came out from hiding to enjoy the fresh breeze and the warmth of the sunshine.

Finn turned to Charmzy and placed his hand on his son's shoulder, his smile gentle. You've done more than I ever could, Charmzy. You've restored the balance."

As the spirits of Ciaran and Lucy appeared beside Finn, their faces glowing with pride, his father's form began to fade.

"No, wait!" Charmzy cried, reaching out.

Finn shook his head. "It's time for me to go, my son. You're the guardian now. Use the power wisely." Charmzy ran into his father's arms for one last embrace. With a final proud smile, Finn, Ciaran, and Lucy dissolved into light, their spirits ascending into the sky.

Charmzy stood staring into the beautiful sky. "I will, father," he whispered. "I promise."

As the last traces of darkness faded, King Olaf, Chelsea, Thunderbolt, Cloveris, Ralsky, Crumbzy, and Gramal gathered around Charmzy, their faces shining with satisfaction and relief.

"We did it," Ralsky said, a grin spreading across his face.

"We did," Charmzy agreed softly. He looked up at the rainbow, now a perfect arc of color stretching across the sky. The rainbow blazed brighter and stronger, a pillar of unified light.

All of a sudden, a magnetic light lifted from the center of the rainbow.

"Oh my, what is it now?" Ralsky said with exhaustion.

It was Angel Christel, an enigma of peace emerging as a being of pure, radiant energy. Her presence alone brought thousands of flowers into bloom and creatures out to play.

In a tender voice, she said, "You have done what no other could, Charmzy. You and your companions have given of yourselves, reflecting the true essence of the rainbow—selflessness, unity, and love—because you chose to put others above your own desires."

With a wave from the angel's hand, the energy of the rainbow flared, stripping Madison and Winfred of their power. They screamed in defeat as the rainbow's light swept them away within their new steel cage, trapped in a dark prison of their own making.

Angel Christel placed a hand on each one of Charmzy's companions, strengthening their bonds. "Because of your sacrifices, the rainbow's power is restored. The Celestial Realm and the human world are once more in perfect harmony and unity. The realms are safe—not through a single act, but through the purity of your hearts."

She turned to Charmzy, her hand glowing softly as she pressed it over his chest. "You are its guardian now, Charmzy. Its protector."

Angel Christel's gaze shifted to Cloveris, her eyes softening with warmth. She placed a glowing hand on his face. "You, Cloveris, are more than just a descendant of the Clovers. You are a living testament to their legacy, the last child of the rainbow. Your courage and heart have rekindled the bond between realms, just as your ancestors once did."

The light around her hand flickered like dancing clover leaves, leaving a small, radiant mark on his shoulder—a clover symbol glowing with the hues of the rainbow and, in her left palm, a clover seedling.

"Carry their strength within you," she whispered. "The light of the Clovers will be your guide, even when hope seems dim. Tend to your new seedling and rebuild the house of Clovers."

Angel Christel turned, her radiant white dress billowing like mist as she stepped onto the arch of the rainbow. With a soft shimmer, she vanished into its colors, leaving only a faint trail of light in her wake.

Where the rainbow's glow touched the earth, something glittered. It was pure, radiant gold, shimmering with the essence of its magic.

"The treasure at the end of the rainbow," Cloveris said, his voice hushed in awe.

"But it's more than just gold," Charmzy murmured, a smile tugging at his lips. "It's a promise of hope, of balance. A reminder that even in the deepest darkness, the light will always return."

The End

About the Author

Michelle LeBron, a self-published author, takes pride in her book Charmzy, which originated from her initial creative writing course. The manuscript, once unfinished and carried for years, was completed with inspiration from her three children and mother. Possessing an entrepreneurial spirit and a zeal for creativity, she aspires for Charmzy to spread enchanting joy on every page.